THE SIEGE

✝✝✝✝✝✝

THE SIEGE

GRAHAM PETRIE

Published by
Soho Press, Inc.
853 Broadway
New York, NY 10003

Library of Congress Cataloging-in-Publication Data

Petrie, Graham.
The Siege/Graham Petrie.
p. cm.
ISBN 1-56947-076-6
I. Title.
PR9199.3.P453S58   1996
813'.54—dc20   95-9076
                                          CIP

Book design by Ilisha Helfman
Composition by The Sarabande Press
Manufactured in the United States
10 9 8 7 6 5 4 3 2 1

✝⊙ CATHY

THE SIEGE

✝✝✝✝✝✝

·Oᴨᴇ

The first thing they saw on entering the room was a large framed photograph hanging on the wall at the head of the bed. Half a dozen men smiled happily into the camera, one of them resting his chin on folded arms that were propped on the handle of a large two-handed saw. They were grouped round another man, lying on a bench, trussed up tightly with a rope. The face of the man on the bench was hidden behind the body of one of those in the foreground.

The landlord smiled proudly when he saw them looking at it. He walked over to stand beside the photograph. "Me," he said, tapping himself on the chest and then touching the figure of the man holding the saw. "My brother," he went on, pointing to the man standing beside him. "My other brother. My cousin. My uncle. And some friends. It was taken twenty years ago, during the war."

Which war? Roger wondered. There have been so many of them here. "And the other man?" he asked. "The one on the bench." Dorothy translated for him, but the landlord understood and replied in English: "A traitor. An informer. Some worthless scum."

Roger cleared his throat. "And what did you do to him?" he asked.

The man made a sawing motion with his hands. "This," he said. "Cut him in half." He smiled, as if inviting their approval.

"How could you—?" Roger began, but Dorothy motioned for him to be silent. "Thank you very much," she said. "The room looks lovely. We'll let you know if we need anything." The landlord nodded and withdrew.

"It's disgusting," Roger said. "The first thing I'm going to do is to take this down." But once again she stopped him. "Don't. You'll just offend him. He seems quite proud of it. It was probably all just a joke anyway, staged for the camera. Once the photo was taken, they probably all went off to the tavern for a drink."

"I doubt it. There have been thousands of atrocities like that here, and not all thirty years ago either, as you well know.

"I can't sleep with that thing hanging over my head," he went on irritably, as if provoked by the silence that followed. "Why don't we compromise, take it down while we're in the room and put it up again when we go out?"

"If you want." But that was no help either; the room, far from lovely to begin with, seemed even bleaker and more desolate without the photo. The discoloured space where it had hung stared at him accusingly and, no matter where he tried to place the picture, face turned to the wall, he still saw it clearly enough. Finally he gave up and replaced it.

"I don't know why you're so blasé about it all. Didn't your parents leave here because they couldn't stand the violence any longer? That man tied up there could be related to you."

4

She made no reply and continued unpacking their things and putting them away. "Look," she said, taking something out of a drawer. "A guidebook."

"Probably full of photos like this one. Local atrocities through the ages. A complete pictorial record."

She pushed the drawer closed and turned to face him. "You didn't *need* to come here," she said quietly. "Nobody forced you."

"*Someone* had to look after you. It was a crazy idea to come here anyway, the way things are at the moment. I'm surprised they even let us enter the country."

"I can look after myself. You can go back if you want to."

"Of course I don't want to. It's just—" He left the sentence unfinished and walked over to the window. "It's certainly beautiful here," he acknowledged. "The hills and the lake. Do you think you'll recognise the house you were born in?"

"It wasn't *all* that primitive here, even thirty-odd years ago. I was born in the hospital. The house we lived in probably doesn't exist any longer, though I'm going to look for it. I remember it as being huge, in a wilderness of a garden full of fruit trees. Maybe it really wasn't all that big, I was only five at the time. And then my parents became 'enemies of the people' and we had to leave."

"Was that the same hospital they shelled last year and killed half the patients? There were gory pictures in all the newspapers and on TV."

"I expect so. It was probably the only one." It was time to change the subject. "Why don't we see if there's anything to eat?"

There were plenty of restaurants, few of them inviting. They chose one at random, where Dorothy interpreted the menu for him and ordered. Roger found the meat tough and almost inedible; he gave up halfway through and pushed the plate away. Dorothy, who had already finished hers, quickly ate the remainder of his.

"How can you *do* that?" he marvelled. "And still keep all your teeth?"

"This isn't a culinary paradise, you know. You're going to get very hungry if you refuse to eat what you're offered."

"I'd rather starve." He pushed his chair away from the table and turned to look out of the window. He took out a cigarette and lit it, then noticed her grimace of disapproval. "Sorry. Force of habit when under stress. I keep thinking of that photo."

"You know why I don't like it—I don't want you to die young. And it really bothers me while I'm eating."

You're not eating, he thought, you've finished.

At home he would go outside for his after-dinner smoke and he automatically offered this now.

"You don't need to."

"It's all right, I could do with a stroll. You sit here and drink your coffee. I'll be back in ten minutes."

It was nine o'clock and getting dark. A few street lights were on, but most were shattered and twisted from the shelling of a few months ago. Little seemed to have been done to clear up the damage: potholes in the street, broken or boarded-up windows, the scars of bullets on the facades of buildings, houses and shops without roofs or walls. People hurried past furtively, silently, heads averted as if deliberately avoiding him. There was hardly any traffic. He began to feel uneasy and wondered if he should turn back. It could be dangerous, especially if he got lost in all those narrow, winding streets. So far he had managed to keep a clear idea of direction, but he had probably gone far enough by now.

He was startled by a touch on his arm and whirled round to see a woman standing in a doorway. She wore a brightly coloured headscarf and a shapeless, gaudily patterned dress; though her face was shrouded in darkness, he sensed that she was young. He shook his head, declining what he assumed was an invitation, but her fingers tightened on his arm and she tried to drag him towards her. He pulled himself free and stepped back to look at her; he could see her face now, youthful and pinched by poverty and hunger. She made another grab at him, without moving from the doorway, and he groped in his pocket for some coins and thrust them into her hand. She glanced contemptuously at them, muttered something that he failed to understand, threw them at his feet and spat on them. Frightened that she might attack him or call for assistance, he turned and walked rapidly away, forcing himself not to run. For a moment he thought he had lost his bearings, but he quickly came to a street that he recognised from the shattered window of what had once been a dressmaker's, still inhabited by the forlorn corpses of naked mannequins, twisted into bizarre angles or lying sprawled on the ground. He breathed more easily and slackened his pace and soon came to the restaurant, where he was surprised to see Dorothy talking animatedly to a young man who had taken the seat that Roger had vacated.

As soon as she saw him, she switched to English and introduced him: "My husband, Roger. And this is Luigi, who happens to be exactly the person I was planning to contact tomorrow. He's the assistant curator of the museum."

Roger took the hand offered him and shook it briefly. "I don't know about you," he told Dorothy, "but I'm heading for bed.

It's been a long day and I'm tired." After a moment's hesitation she nodded and said goodbye to Luigi, arranging to meet him at the same spot the next morning.

"You weren't very polite. You might at least have spoken to him."

"Why should I? He was probably trying to pick you up anyway. How did you come to meet him?"

"Don't be silly. I must be almost twice his age."

"You haven't told me how you met him."

"Coincidence." She was reluctant to fuel his jealousy, for Luigi had indeed accosted her under the pretext of asking for a match. "I asked him if he knew when the museum opened. And it turned out that he worked there." She wondered how old Luigi thought her; it was common, she knew, for the local women to age rapidly once they had passed thirty, and he perhaps assumed that she was several years younger than she really was. Though she felt oddly flattered at the idea, it would be unwise, under the circumstances, to encourage any romantic interest on his part.

"And you're seeing him again tomorrow?"

"Of course. That's why I came here. You should come too."

"I'll see."

Despite his plea of tiredness, he showed no sign of going to bed once they reached the hotel. First he insisted on a drink in the hotel bar, then he said he would stay downstairs and catch up on some of the work he had brought with him: "Can't let everything slide completely for three weeks, you know."

"I thought you were supposed to be on holiday."

"A lawyer is never on holiday. You should know that by now. You go to bed. You must be tired, you did a lot of driving today."

She had no desire to argue and, once he had collected his briefcase from their room and kissed her goodnight, she began to get ready for bed. But she found it impossible to sleep and got up again and went over to the open window, leaning on the sill to savour the cool night air. She could see a corner of the lake and also the hills that came down almost to the shore, hemming the town in on all sides. It was from those hills that the inhabitants had been sporadically and randomly bombarded for several weeks by attackers who made no attempt to seize the town, which they could have done easily enough, preferring simply to create havoc and terror, and occasionally infiltrate snipers who took a morbid pleasure in singling out the most harmless and defenceless targets—old men and women, children, even at times babies.

Mark had been killed in the same way all those years ago— a bullet out of nowhere as he straddled a branch of a pear tree and was about to throw a pear down to her. She wondered once again if it was wise to have come here, stirring up painful memories, but she had work to do, an opportunity that might never be repeated. And, by all reports, the situation was stable for the moment: The U.N.-enforced truce had held for six months now and life had regained a kind of normality. Roger, who had followed reports of the fighting assiduously, had refused at first to allow her to come and finally reluctantly agreed on condition that he accompany her, to "protect" her. Even so, it was only the fact of her dual nationality that had persuaded the authorities to permit them to enter.

Finally she closed the window and went back to bed, but, before turning out the light, glanced through the guidebook that she had found earlier. It had sections in English, French and German and was several years out of date, making no mention of the recent discovery of the frescoes. It also scrupulously omitted all reference to the bitter ethnic and religious conflicts of the past few decades, preferring to concentrate on heroic battles, deeds of personal valour, and glamorous acts of banditry in the distant past. The English section was written in the fractured syntax and erratic vocabulary that are always good for light relief in newspaper travel supplements, though she wondered how well English and American tourist agencies coped with providing guidebooks in Ukrainian or Japanese. Perhaps they never even attempted it, assuming, no doubt correctly, that everyone spoke English now in any case. After a few minutes, she gave up the struggle to decipher it and prepared to go to sleep.

Roger found himself alone in the bar. Although he had brought his papers down, he made no attempt to consult them and had never intended to do so in the first place. He wanted time to think things over; he was uneasy and needed to reassess the situation. If the decision had been left to him, neither of them would be here at all; but Dorothy had become unnaturally fixated on these frescoes once she had heard about their discovery and there had been no way of stopping her. She was the ideal person to examine them, she insisted: They fell exactly into her area of expertise, they had been found in the town she had been born in, she spoke the language perfectly. As she obviously could not be allowed to go on her own, he had finally agreed on a maximum of three weeks, during her summer vacation, with the firm understanding that if there was the slightest sign of the truce being violated, they would leave immediately.

It was not really this that was worrying him, he realised, for, now that they were here, he was prepared to make the best of it and the visit could indeed turn out to be very interesting. It was her meeting with Luigi that disturbed him and the obvious pleasure that she had taken in his company. She was still an attractive woman, with a good figure and that wild tangle of blond hair that had first drawn him to her; men tended to gravitate towards her in a way that he found upsetting, even though he was quite sure that things never went further than a mild flirtation. In the early days of their marriage he had protested against her easy acceptance of this admiration and the close friendships that she enjoyed with several male colleagues, both married and single. She had paid little heed to this and had made it clear that, as he had nothing to worry about, she had no intention of changing her style of life to allay his suspicions. He continued to worry nevertheless, for his own experience had always been that friendship between a man and woman was impossible: It inevitably turned into something else.

No doubt Luigi was harmless enough, with his sallow, undernourished complexion, the old-fashioned "granny" glasses and his already thinning hair, but he decided to play it safe by imposing his presence on them for the first two or three days at least, to make sure that the other man got the message. After that, he could get on with his own concerns, whatever they turned out to be.

A woman had drifted into the bar and seated herself at a table close to him. In the dim light it was difficult to make out her features clearly, but she seemed middle-aged and heavily made-up. When she caught him looking at her, she smiled and tilted her head slightly in a gesture of invitation. He smiled back, shook his head and left the room.

He found it difficult to get to sleep, with that damned photograph hanging over his head. What kind of person would keep that as a souvenir and show it off proudly to guests? He thought again of taking it down and this time hiding it under the bed, but he knew that, wherever he put it, he would go on seeing it, the six men happily anticipating the brutal slaughter of another human being. Against his will, he found himself imagining what it would be like to be the victim and how long it would take to die, and how painfully. Perhaps they lengthened it by slow dismemberment, first an arm, then a leg and only finally the *coup de grace* across the neck or the middle. He tried to think of something else, but found himself visualising another photograph, from a book he had read recently, this time of an Australian prisoner of war, kneeling on the ground, arms bound behind his back, neck stretched forward in resignation as a Japanese soldier stood poised beside him with sword raised. And then another picture from the same book, a drawing this time, of an emaciated man tied in crucifix position to a tree, with the caption underneath: "Jap torture in Siam. This man was later beaten to death with a sledgehammer." Did that proceed by stages too, he wondered, the bones of the legs, then the knees, then the arms, or was there just one merciful smash to the head or the stomach? In Idi Amin's Uganda, prisoners were forced to beat one another to death with sledgehammers, each man acting first as executioner, then as victim, the survivor being finished off by one of the guards; there too it must have been kinder to be cruel, to hit hard and true rather than trying to soften the blow.

The manacles were removed from his wrist and he was handed the sledgehammer. The barrel of an assault rifle poked him hard in the ribs, urging him to hurry up. The floor of the cell was slippery with blood and fragments of bone and brains; he had difficulty keeping his balance. It was very dark and he could not make out the face of the man he was about to kill, though he knew that he was a friend, someone he loved and had known since childhood. "Forgive me," he whispered. He stood there, the hammer raised shoulder-high, and wondered why he just didn't swing it wildly, accounting for at least one or two of the guards before they shot him down. As if guessing his intention, those nearest him shuffled a few feet away, keeping their weapons trained on him. "Hurry up," one of them ordered. It would be easier for *him* to die this way, he thought, but how would it help the man tied here on the bench? Someone else would be made to kill him, someone who would not weep with pity as he struck, as he was doing now. The only hope would be for all the prisoners to act together, rushing the guards and forcing them to shoot them all and so dying by their own choice and with some dignity, but it was far too late for that now.

There was a sudden switch of place and now it was he who was the victim. "Hurry up," he begged, but the men were enjoying themselves far too much to bring it all to an end so soon. They stood round him, passing the bottle from hand to hand, joking, insulting him, telling him exactly what they planned to do with his friends and his family when they caught them. One of them leaned over him, his mouth full of liquid and spat it expertly in his face.

"Don't waste good liquor," the landlord said. "Just piss on him instead." He followed up his suggestion, laughing raucously, and the other men imitated him.

"All right," one of them said, "let's do it now."

"Wait," the landlord ordered, "we'll take a photograph first." They rearranged themselves around him, smiling proudly into the camera. "Let's get on with it, then," the landlord said. "You take the other side." Roger screamed as he felt the first rip of the blades into his flesh and blood streamed everywhere, over his stomach, the sheets, the bed, covering the floor of the room.

He felt someone shaking him, tugging at his shoulders, and saw Dorothy's face close to his, her eyes wide with anxiety. "What's wrong? What were you screaming about?" He struggled into a sitting position, shielding his eyes against the light that she had switched on. "A nightmare. That fucking photo." His pyjamas were soaked with sweat and he got out of bed to strip them off, then walked over to the window, opening it to let the cool air flow in against his skin. It was still quite dark, though he could distinguish the outline of the hills against the first signs of dawn, and a band of moonlight lay across the lake.

"We'll have to get rid of it," he said. "Or else get out of here and go somewhere else."

"There's nowhere else we can go. This is the only half-decent hotel. Or, at any rate, the only one left standing."

"A private house, then. Rent a room there. Or change to another room here. But then that's probably got its own characteristic décor, people beating one another to death with sledgehammers. I'm beginning to hate this place already."

She looked at him in puzzlement. "Come back to bed. Try to get some sleep." He shook his head, but returned nevertheless, kicking his sodden pyjamas aside but too tired to search for clean ones.

"There," she said, stroking him, "you'll feel better now." He snuggled closer to her, enjoying her warmth, settling into the familiar contours of her body. He started to caress her in turn and, sleepily and clumsily, they began to make love.

He took the photo down first thing in the morning and put it under the bed. "I refuse to look at it any longer. I'll decide what to do about it later."

When they asked about breakfast a sullen-looking maid told them they could have coffee and bread; if they wanted anything else, they would have to go elsewhere. "Charming," he said. "Such old-fashioned hospitality. Let's go out."

They went to the restaurant of the previous evening, but found that it had little more to offer. "Coffee and bread, then. Why not live it up while we can? What time are you meeting Leonardo?"

"Luigi. Around ten o'clock. What are you going to do?"

Her tenderness and concern of last night had made him ashamed of his petty jealousy and he no longer felt any need to impose himself on her this morning.

"I don't know. Maybe do some work. Or just wander around, see what there is to see."

"There's not very much, I'm afraid. Except the museum and the church."

"Where your frescoes are?"

"Yes. But Sister Margaret's journals are in the museum."

"I'll maybe look in at the church, then."

She said that she would wait at the restaurant for Luigi and they arranged to meet for lunch. He went back to the hotel, determined to force a confrontation with the landlord over the photo, but he was intercepted in the foyer by a seedy-looking man wearing an ill-fitting suit, a collarless shirt blotched with stains from coffee or some other liquid and a hat that he apparently never removed.

"Mr. Everest?"

"Yes?"

"I am Adam, a reporter for the local newspaper. I wonder if you could give me an interview?"

"What on earth for?"

"You are here to examine the frescoes, yes?"

"I am here to examine the frescoes, no. You're thinking of my wife."

The man looked puzzled. "Your wife?"

"She's the art historian, not me. I'm just a poor lawyer."

"And your wife, where is she?"

He looked at his watch. "At this moment she is meeting someone called Luigi, from the museum. I'll be seeing her for lunch. I'll ask her then if she wants to be interviewed."

"Perhaps I could meet her too, at lunch?"

"I don't think so. She may not care to be disturbed. She may not even want to be interviewed. Let me ask her first."

Adam looked disappointed, then brightened up. "Perhaps I could interview you instead. I have set aside the morning for it."

Roger was about to refuse, but he had nothing better to do and the man's eagerness amused him. "Half an hour, then," he conceded.

Adam led the way into the bar. "Let me offer you a brandy. My paper will pay."

"It's a bit early for that. I'll take coffee."

Adam pulled a tattered notebook from one pocket and a pencil stub from another. He propped the notebook on his knee, licked the point of the pencil and stared at Roger expectantly.

"Aren't you going to ask me any questions?"

"No, it is better if you speak. About your wife, about yourself."

This is ridiculous, Roger thought. "Let me ask *you* something first," he said. "About the landlord here."

Adam looked uneasy. "What about the landlord?"

"There's a photograph in our room, of some men about to saw another man in half. Is it genuine? Did they actually do it?"

"I don't understand."

"Come upstairs. I'll show you." He drained his coffee, swallowing some of the bitter grounds by mistake, while Adam gulped down his brandy.

The room had been made up and the photo rehung above

the bed. "There," Roger said. "The landlord says that's him, holding the saw, and that they went ahead and killed the man."

"It's possible. I don't know for sure. Terrible things have taken place here."

"Surely it's a famous incident? People would know about it if it really happened?"

"It's not so special. Why worry about it? If it did happen, it happened long ago. There are worse things going on now. If you want, I show you."

Roger ignored the offer, barely hearing it, for the landlord now appeared in the doorway. He looked at them in silence.

"I want that thing removed," Roger said abruptly, pointing to the photo. "It's giving me nightmares."

The man gave a stiff, formal bow. "As you wish. I will tell the maid to take it down."

Roger would have preferred the man do it himself, but he seemed finally to have made his point. "See that it's done," he added severely. The man nodded.

"Do you want to continue with the interview?" Adam asked, when the landlord had left.

"All right. Let's go back downstairs. And this time I think I *will* have a brandy."

"It was quite remarkable," Luigi said. "The shell struck the church and blew away the whole wall that had hidden them for centuries. And not a speck of damage."

"They're wonderful. And they haven't faded at all."

"That must have something to do with the way they were walled up soon after they were completed. The church hierarchy hated them, you know." She nodded.

"What's surprising is that they weren't simply destroyed or

whitewashed over," he continued. "There must have been a reason for this; perhaps Margaret's journals will give us a clue. For centuries everyone thought they *had* been destroyed or even that she had lied about painting them or somehow imagined that she had. The only real evidence for their existence was in her journals and much of what she wrote there was thought to be sheer fantasy. Sexual fantasies in particular."

"I'm surprised they didn't suppress them too."

"They made selective use of them in what they published, choosing the parts that were conventional moralising and devotional exercises, though some of these seem to me rather suspect. They even included some of the sexual passages, which they decided to interpret as religious allegories. They just ignored the rest. Her writing's often almost impossible to read in any case."

"Has anyone else come to see them? The frescoes, I mean. Outsiders like me."

"No, you're the first since that journalist who was here and wrote about them. The fighting was still going on then and I suppose most people were afraid to come here."

It was only a small paragraph or two, hidden away in the middle of a longer report on the civil war that Roger, daily following its progress, had brought to her notice. She would probably have paid little attention to it herself but for the coincidence that they had been discovered in her birthplace. She had contacted the journalist, but he could tell her little more than what was in the article: that they probably dated from the first half of the sixteenth century, were in a state of perfect preservation and local tradition maintained that they had been painted by a nun.

She might still have left it at that, except that the idea of going back "home," as her parents had continued to refer to it, intrigued her. They had always refused to return, claiming that it was too dangerous, but now it was "their" side that was in control, however temporarily, and the risk was much smaller. And perhaps it was time too to face up to the trauma of her brother's death, the sight of Mark dropping from the tree to land directly at her feet with half his head blown away, the pear he had just picked rolling slowly away from his open hand. Her parents had never spoken of it, perhaps deluding themselves that their silence would enable her to forget. And, after the first few weeks, in the excitement and terror of moving and then settling into a new country and a new language, the memory had faded or been suppressed. But she had never actually forgotten what she had seen and every so often it would surface, as if illuminated by a sudden flash of lightning, and then recede again into darkness.

"They *are* frightening," she agreed, realising that Luigi was staring at her expectantly and belatedly answering his half-heard question. "I can see why people didn't like them. Yet they accepted Bosch and Breughel."

"Men," he said.

"That's the easy explanation and there's probably some truth in it: If a woman's going to paint at all, she should do something uplifting and maternal. Which is what most of these paintings appear to be, until you look more closely and see that they're really full of death and torture."

"How long do you have here and what are your plans?"

"My husband's allowed me three weeks. He's got to be back then for his work. But I could stay on longer if I had to; my term doesn't start till September, that's five weeks away. I should probably begin by taking lots of photos and then look at the journals. I don't suppose there's such a thing as a photocopying machine around?"

"Even if there was, my boss wouldn't allow you to copy the journals. They're too fragile."

"I thought *you* were the boss?"

"I'm just the assistant curator, a very minor figure. To tell you the truth, though, my boss is extremely lazy and leaves it to me to do all the work. That's why I answered your letters and am looking after you. Now, if you have everything you need, I have other things to attend to and I'll leave you to your photographing."

Roger felt a stab of annoyance at seeing Luigi sitting there in the restaurant beside her: The fellow seemed to be becoming a nuisance already.

"I asked Luigi to join us," she explained, unnecessarily. He nodded.

"How's it been going?"

"Fine. It's very dark inside the church, however. Luigi's been a great help, rustling up extra lights for me. He's also promised to introduce me to his boss, who spends all day lying on a sofa, eating chocolates and listening to ancient 78 RPM opera records."

He grunted and picked up the menu. "Tell me what I should order as long as it's not what I had last night."

"The fish is very good here," Luigi offered. "It's a specialty and comes fresh from the lake."

"I don't like fish." Dorothy opened her mouth to contradict him, then closed it abruptly. "Is there anything with pork or chicken?"

"Yes," she said frostily. "Both."

"I'll take pork, then. But tell them to cook it properly this time."

She gave the order and several moments of silence followed. "Tell me what *you've* been doing," she said at last.

He told her about Adam and his desire to interview her. "He seems harmless enough, not all that bright. I told him you were a big media star back home, even had your own TV programme. He was very impressed."

"Why did you tell him that?"

"Why not? Gives him something to write about."

"But now I'll have to tell him the truth."

Luigi had been listening to this in puzzlement. "Do you mean you *don't* have your own TV programme?" he asked.

"Of course not. I'm a minor academic from a minor university. I've only been interviewed once in my life, on a local radio station, and that was to do with cookery."

"A *very* minor university," Roger added. "Almost invisible."

"There's nothing wrong with it. It's treated me pretty well."

He made no response to this and said little more during the meal. Luigi seemed intimidated by the hostile atmosphere and excused himself once they were finished, saying that he had work to do.

Roger said he would come to the church with her and look at the frescoes. "At least I've got rid of that photo," he told her. "I made the landlord take it away."

She ignored this. "Why did you behave like that?" she asked angrily. "You were *very* rude to him."

"No, I wasn't. I hardly even spoke to him."

"That's what I mean. He's really very nice."

"I don't like him. What's he always hanging around you for?"

She sighed. "He's my liaison here. He can give me a lot of useful information."

"Maybe liaison's the right word," he muttered.

"What do you mean by that?"

"Nothing. He just seems very keen on you, that's all."

"Look," she said, stopping in the middle of the street. "This is becoming ridiculous. I've got a lot on my mind and I don't need to be bothered with your stupid jealousy."

"All right," he said. "Sorry. I won't mention him again. Let's look at the frescoes."

"They look normal enough to me," he said. "Aren't they the standard themes of the period: lots of the Virgin and Child, the Infant Christ, God Surrounded by Angels, Saint X and Saint Y? There're the usual gruesome ones, of course—Saint Sebastian and people being martyred in nasty ways like being roasted on grills. And hell doesn't look like much of a rest cure. Is that what they were worried about—a woman treating that kind of subject?"

"Maybe, but that's not all there is to it. I don't know enough about it yet, I'll have to read Margaret's journals. But just look at them more closely."

"Well, that Virgin looks rather plump and homely—not a Raphael or Fra Angelico type at all. And the Massacre of the Innocents is pretty powerful, with the little bodies scattered all around and the heads neatly piled up in a pyramid. The mothers look genuinely distressed by it all; there's a real sense of suffering."

"And in the background life goes on; Herod and the priests—in the church robes of her own time—feasting and enjoying themselves."

"But that was normal practice then, wasn't it? To set the biblical stories in the present."

"Yes. But it's still a pretty strong statement all the same. It implicates the contemporary church in the violence, perhaps even suggests that they too would try to kill Christ if they had the chance."

"I suppose this one's Judith and—what was his name?"

"Holofernes."

"I wouldn't like to meet her on a dark night, especially holding that sword."

"Don't you think she's been raped?"

"What?"

"Look at her clothes, they've obviously been torn and there are bloodstains over her thighs."

"Could be from that head she's holding."

"Maybe. And look at him, he's totally naked, except for that sheet covering his private parts. That's not usual."

"I don't remember the story very well, but I'm sure it wasn't about a rape."

"Perhaps that's how she wanted to interpret it. Look at Susanna and the Elders, it's completely different from the usual versions, where Susanna faces the viewer and you get a good look at her naked body, especially the breasts. Here she faces away, towards the Elders, and all you can see is her back. And just look at their faces—wizened, drooling, depraved, syphilitic. That one there who looks like a monk has obviously got an erection."

"I don't like it. I think it's ugly."

"Maybe it's meant to be ugly. Maybe you're meant not to like it. Sexual assault isn't pleasant."

He sighed. "Just *looking* at her is *assault*?"

"In these circumstances, yes."

"I'll look at the rest on my own, I think. Without the feminist commentary."

"If you want." She began to set up her tripod and camera.

He wandered round the rest of the room. Another life-size

23

picture of an angry-looking woman disposing of a man, this time with a large nail in his forehead, while straddling him in an unpleasantly aggressive sexual manner. At first sight, in fact, it looked as though they were actually making love. He began to feel uneasy, as though he too were being attacked. But then Dorothy would probably tell him—indeed *had* often told him—that that was how a woman felt, in a room full of nudes painted by men or the classical rape scenes—Lucretia, the Sabine women, Leda, Europa. There were none of these here, of course, not in a church, but this woman—Margaret—would probably have found a way to twist them around if she'd been allowed to use them.

He stopped at a large painting of Christ in glory, surrounded by a dozen or so smaller scenes from his life—Nativity, baptism, various miracles, clearing the money changers from the temple, entry into Jerusalem, Gethsemane, trial before Pilate, Crucifixion, Resurrection. One of them depicted the marriage at Cana, with a bride and groom, family members, guests, someone serving wine. In the background people were carrying out household tasks—feeding hens, milking cows, chopping wood. He was struck by the sight of two men sawing a huge log on a trestle with a double-handed saw; strangely, a priest was standing beside them with his hand raised in benediction. Examining it more closely, he realised that they were cutting a man in half. Forgetting his recent resentment, he called for Dorothy to come over.

"Yes," she said, "I'd noticed that. It seems to be part of a long and honourable tradition around here. Except that, if you look properly, you'll see it's not a man, it's a woman, and she has exactly the bride's features. And one of the men is the bridegroom and the other is the man standing to her left in the foreground—presumably her father. And the priest is the same one who is marrying them. My theory is that it's a deliberate sub-version of the 'happy marriage' idea—the bride as a victim or sacrifice, controlled and destroyed by the men, with the church's blessing."

"Your Sister Margaret must have been sick. I think I've had enough of this."

"Maybe she thought it was her society that was sick. And you wouldn't mind if it was by Bosch. He's full of images far worse than this."

"I'm going," he said. "And I don't think I'll be back in a hurry."

He felt angry both with himself and with her. He had always tried to support her and show sympathy for her ideas, but in recent weeks she'd been getting worse and worse, and it looked as though what she was doing here was going to put her right over the edge, taking the side of this irrationally antimale artist at every opportunity. If she felt like this about marriage—that she was some sort of victim—why had she married him? But that was unreasonable, she was talking about the past, when many women *were* sacrificed in marriage, for economic, politi-cal or social reasons. There was no need to apply it to their own situation.

He realised that he needed a drink and made his way back to the hotel. At least there would be someone there who could understand English. What on earth was he going to do with himself for the next three weeks, in this total backwater where he knew no one and couldn't speak a word of the language? He had hoped vaguely that he could somehow keep in touch with home and do some work while he was here, but he had seen enough already to realise that it was ludicrous to expect to find

"It's all right. I have an appointment already. My girlfriend."

"It's not that Roger's really hostile. It's more that he's shy. He takes some time to warm up to strangers." Especially if they're men, she thought, and seem to like me. "You'd think a lawyer would be more used to meeting people."

"It happens. I'm shy too."

She decided to go back to the hotel, have a shower and change. No doubt Roger would find his way back in due course. She hoped he wouldn't go on being a bore, jealous and bad-tempered. His reactions this afternoon had been rather unusual; normally he was much more open-minded and willing to listen to her ideas. If he carried on like this, it would probably be better for him to go home: He would be a lot happier there, back at work, and he had only come here out of a misguided sense of chivalry. Maybe not all that misguided though, she thought, glancing up at the mountains. The reports that had come out of here a year ago were pretty horrific and it was easy enough to cut the town off completely from the outside world. Rumour had it that the terrorists were still encamped up there, biding their time before starting up again. "Terrorists" or "bandits" was what the townspeople called them, of course; in their own eyes they were fighters for justice and freedom.

She would have to find time while she was here to look around the town and try to identify some of the landmarks—if they still existed—that her parents had mentioned in the infrequent reminiscences they had shared with her. They had insisted that she learn the language and read the literature, but had otherwise spoken only rarely about the country and its history—and then mainly in terms of regret for a lost and idyllic past and anger at an alien present. And their house too: She would have to try to find that, though she had only the haziest recollection of its appearance and its surroundings and these had probably changed beyond all recognition. The wall of silence that had prevented talk of her childhood had lasted right up to her parents' deaths and she did not even know the address; but the town was still small enough that she might encounter something in her wanderings that would trigger the right chain of associations. Perhaps she could persuade Roger to accompany her on her search, in the evenings.

She was surprised to notice that, though he had said that he had got rid of the photo, it was nevertheless still there. Or had it perhaps been removed and then rehung? She studied it more closely as she undressed. It was easy enough to recognise the landlord; the other men looked like normal, everyday people, relaxing after a hard day's work. One of them held a bottle to his lips and was drinking from it. Ordinary working men, with families and children, about to commit an atrocity. No different from those who had hidden in the hills and deliberately shelled ambulances and picked off doctors and nurses, or had continued to attack refugees *after* they had crossed the border to what should have been safety. The amazing thing, she realised, was that doctors and nurses continued to try to work under these conditions and refused to give up; she doubted that she would have their courage and idealism. Especially when she suspected that the victims would retaliate in kind if they gained the upper hand.

She heard someone fumbling at the door handle and automatically grabbed at a towel to cover herself. It was only Roger, however, though he looked unusually pale and walked unsteadily as if he had had too much to drink.

"What's the matter?" she asked.

He shook his head without answering and slumped down on the bed. After a moment he looked up at her. "I'm not drunk, if that's what you're thinking, though I probably *have* had rather too much of that poisonous brandy. It's all the fault of that bastard Adam."

"The journalist?"

"Journalist. Tour guide. Specialist in local atrocities. Amateur psychiatrist. He plays a lot of roles."

"And?"

He stretched out at full length, his head propped against a pillow. "Well, he waylaid me as usual and we had a few drinks and then he said he wanted to show me something he knew I'd be interested in. I wasn't sure what he was talking about, but I went along." He looked up at her. "Don't get the wrong idea. I wasn't hoping for a live sex show or anything like that. I just didn't know what to expect."

"Go on."

"It was a museum of torture. Somewhere in the Old Town. He said it was the only one in the world."

"He's wrong there. There's one in Amsterdam. Or is it The Hague? London, Paris, lots of them."

"I don't know why he thought I would want to go there. He seems to think I'm some kind of sadist, perhaps because I showed him that photo in here." He glanced up automatically and gave a groan of disgust when he realised that the picture was still there. "For Christ's sake! I *told* him to get rid of it."

He groped upward in an attempt to remove it, but she stopped him.

"Leave it for now. It's not important, we'll dispose of it later. Go on with what you were telling me."

He leaned back against the pillow. "Well, when I discovered what it was, I said I didn't want to go inside, but he said it would be educational, historical; it would help me understand what was going on here."

He grimaced. "It was worse than anything you could imagine. The first room was full of drawings, prints and woodcuts—torture through the ages—all of them very detailed and graphic. There were written descriptions too; he began to translate them for me but I told him to stop, I couldn't stomach it. Yet the horrible thing was that really I was fascinated by them: I wanted him to continue, even though I said I didn't. Do you understand what I mean?"

"I think so. It's a fairly common experience, unfortunately."

"The next room was the torture instruments themselves, going back for several centuries. He started to explain them all to me with great gusto, exactly how they worked, the kind of pain they inflicted, how long it took to die if that's what they wanted to do to you. Sometimes it took days. You've no idea what people are capable of doing, the ingenuity, the inventiveness, the cruelty. I hadn't anyway, not to that extent. There was one—" He stopped and shook his head. "Not now. Later perhaps.

"The third room was worse, life-size replicas of these things in action, down to the smallest detail, with wax models of the victims. People being impaled, broken on the wheel, torn apart on the rack, boiled in oil, roasted on spits, flayed alive. All horribly realistic, the contortions of the bodies, the agony on the faces. And Adam as cool as a cucumber, drawing my attention to anything he thought I might have missed." He paused and drew a deep breath.

"The last room was worst of all. Photographs. Not just the preliminaries, like the one here, but when it was actually happening. Mostly from this area, he said, but they'd obtained others—medical experiments from the Nazi concentration camps and the Japanese in Manchuria, the Lubyanka prison in Moscow, the French in Algeria, the Khmer Rouge, Haiti. . . . It seemed to go on forever. He was very proud of these and appeared to think I should appreciate them too. I just took one glance and left. He came running after me, tugging at my sleeve, asking what was wrong, had he offended me in some way. I told him to go to hell and leave me alone and not to bother with interviewing you. Not that he'll pay any attention." He paused again.

"And all the time I was wishing I hadn't been so squeamish, that I'd stayed just a moment or two longer, that I'd looked at some of them more closely. Just for educational purposes, of course." He laughed briefly. "What do you think of that?"

"It's nothing to be ashamed of. We all have something of that in us."

"Not all of us, surely?"

"Except a few saints."

"Like the ones Margaret painted? Being martyred? Some people would say they enjoyed having that done to them, that they deliberately invited it."

"It's one thing to think about these things, even to paint them or write about them, and another to do them. Not everyone is capable of that."

"I wonder."

"I think we should stop talking about this and you should change and have a shower. And then we should eat."

"And this?" He nodded up at the photo. "By comparison with what I saw today, it's pretty harmless. Even endearing."

"We'll take it downstairs with us and give it to the landlord. He can do what he wants with it."

The landlord was nowhere to be found, however. The sullen maid said that he had gone out and agreed reluctantly to put the photo behind the bar and give it to him when he returned.

"I wonder why he was never punished for it," Roger remarked. "If they really did kill that fellow."

"I should think a lot of things go unpunished here. Justice must be rather a rough-and-ready concept. More a question of private vendettas and feuds."

"Isn't he taking a risk, then, reminding everyone of what he did?"

"Maybe he just keeps it to show to strangers like us."

"Could be. For all his expertise in the subject, friend Adam didn't seem to know anything about it."

They agreed to try a different restaurant from the one they had eaten in so far but, as they passed it, they caught sight of Luigi in the company of an attractive red-haired young woman. Luigi noticed them and waved.

"We'll just say hello and go on. That must be his girlfriend." But Luigi looked doubtful when she said they planned to eat elsewhere. "There *is* nowhere else," he said. "Nowhere better, at any rate, I'm afraid."

She glanced at Roger, who shrugged and made no objection to staying. Perhaps the sight of the woman—Eva—had reassured him. Like Luigi she spoke excellent English. She told them that she ran a clothing store: "High fashion, or at least it used to be. Now I sell whatever I can get, mostly secondhand. If there's anything you don't need when you leave, I'll buy it from you."

"What will you have?" Luigi asked. "The fish is good, but your husband—"

"Of course he'll have the fish," Dorothy interrupted. "He loves fish. He was just being awkward this morning." She noticed sourly that Roger was already deep in conversation with Eva and was staring into her eyes with undisguised admiration. Just like him, she thought. Goes berserk if I even talk to a man

33

and then falls head over heels for every available woman he meets, even if she's not available. I hope he doesn't take it too far and cause problems, I need Luigi's help.

When they left, after several bottles of wine and a good deal of brandy— all ordered and paid for by Roger—he seemed contented for the first time since their arrival. "Luigi's not such a bad chap after all," he mused, "and that fish was really good." He paused and cleared his throat. "Eva says that, if I've nothing better to do, she can show me around a bit. She's not all that busy at the moment."

"Wonderful," Dorothy said bleakly.

When they got into bed, Roger put his arm around her and tried to draw her close; but when she turned away he did not persist and, as usual, was quickly asleep. He's unbelievable, she thought bitterly, behaving as if I hadn't noticed. Or perhaps he just doesn't care any longer. Maybe I should just give up now and go home, before it gets any worse. But why? Just to stop him from making a fool of himself, yet again? I've got more important things to do with my life than that.

She would stay, and accomplish what she had come to do. The frescoes were the top priority, but Margaret's journals could be important too and she should get to work on them right away. With time so short, it would be pointless to try to produce an exact translation on the spot; it would be better to get the gist of it down in her own words and hope that later she would have the chance to do a more literal version. If, that is, there was anything worth recording in them to begin with. . . .

The Siege

✠ Margaret ✠

The Duke was halfway across the hall when I rushed forward and threw myself at his feet. His guards swooped on me immediately, but he waved them away. "Let her speak," he ordered. I stood up and brushed the dust from my robe: I would rather talk to him alone, I requested, not in front of all these people. He said he would see me after dinner. The procession swept on.

I resumed my place among the other nuns. "What do you think you're up to?" the Abbess hissed, grabbing my arm and digging her long fingernails so deeply into the flesh that I squealed with pain. "A common little novice like you accosting His Highness. Of course you can't speak to him."

"He said I could," I protested.

"He didn't mean it, he was just trying to avoid a scene. I'll tell him you're hysterical, you often do things like that, it doesn't mean anything." She saw my look of defiance and went on, "Or would you prefer me to have you locked up instead?" I said nothing.

At dinner the Duke sat at the high table with the church dignitaries and the Abbot and the Abbess. The monks sat on one side of the room, we nuns on the other, carefully graded by age and rank. I was right at the bottom, beside the door. I ate very little, trying to nerve myself for another intervention: No doubt he would have me whipped this time, he was well known to be capricious, but I was too desperate to care. When the meal ended and they marched solemnly down the centre of the room, I threw myself in front of him again.

"This is getting to be a habit," he said, recognising me. He burst into laughter at his joke and, after a moment's stunned silence, everyone else joined in, even the Abbess. "I meant I would see you in my chambers."

"The Abbess forbade me," I said. "But I have to speak to you."

"She's crazy," the Abbess shouted, pushing her way forward. "Don't listen to a word she says, Your Highness. She's given us nothing but trouble ever since she came here."

"Please," I begged.

He stretched out his hand and helped me to my feet. Such a mark of favour silenced even the Abbess and she retreated into the background. "Come along with me," he said.

In his chambers he dismissed everyone except two guards, who stood by the doorway. He settled himself in a chair and waved me to a bench a few feet away. "Well?"

I told him everything, as logically as I could. I mentioned my father and reminded the Duke of his long years of loyal service. He nodded at the name and looked at me with new interest. The next part was more difficult, explaining what I was doing here: I thought he might understand, I told him, as it was rumoured that he too had married for love, defying his family's wishes. He frowned at this, displeased at having his private affairs the subject of common gossip. I thought he was about to dismiss me and went on quickly with my story: Not that I had even succeeded in marrying, of course; they caught up with us far too quickly. My eldest brother killed Stefan with his own hand and would have killed me too, if my father had not stopped him. They gave me a choice: Go through with the marriage they had arranged for me or become a nun. I was lucky to *have* the choice, they said, for only a man of exceptional generosity would overlook the scandal I had caused and the indelible stain on my reputation. I told them I would rather die than marry that fat pig and that all he was after was my dowry.

"So you want me to release you from your vows?" the Duke asked. He rested his elbows on the arms of his chair and folded his hands beneath his chin, gazing at me steadily. "You know that's impossible. Not even I can do that."

I told him I was aware of this and it was something entirely different that I wanted. I was my father's only daughter and, after my mother's death, he had shown a particular fondness for me, saying often how much I reminded him of her. For, though they had married to suit their parents, they had come to love each other greatly. I think it was the memory of this that made him seize my brother's arm when his sword was already at my throat, and spare my life. Although he was a warrior, my father was also a man of refinement, he loved poetry and music and painting, and it was a bitter disappointment to him that my brothers were all uncultivated boors with no interests beyond hunting, fighting, drinking and wenching. He saw that I had a talent for artistic matters and devoted himself to my education, hiring the finest tutors and sparing no expense. I loved painting most of all and showed unusual ability—for a woman, as they always said. I mentioned the names of some artists who had taught me and had praised my work, and the Duke nodded in approval.

So now that I was condemned to drag out the rest of my life here, I asked for permission to be at least allowed to paint. There was much that could be done, both in the convent and in the church: What little artwork existed already was of deplorable quality and in an advanced state of disintegration. It would be kinder to plaster it all over and start again. I spoke with enthusiasm of my plans, for I had spent months brooding on them and knew exactly what I wanted to begin with—a huge Christ in glory, surrounded by angels, and kneeling at his feet two men with the features of the Duke himself and the Bishop.

He smiled at this, saying that it was a politic choice and unlikely to meet with much resistance. I said nothing of some of my other plans, the most cherished ones, knowing that they would not meet with such easy approval; but I trusted that, with the Duke on my side, I could put some of them, at least, into effect.

"And all this is for the glory of God, of course," he asked, gazing at me thoughtfully, "and the praise and honour of his saints? I detect no hint of sinful pride, of self-seeking or self-gratification?"

I shook my head vigorously: Nothing could be further from my mind, I assured him. I wished only to elevate and inspire those who saw my work, to direct their thoughts towards eternity and the salvation of their souls.

"I will see what I can do," he said finally, "though I promise nothing. You look tired, however, and hungry. Let me order you some refreshment." I knew better than to refuse: It was the price I had to pay and I had anticipated it. He ordered one of the guards to bring us food and wine, then told them both to withdraw and that he was not to be disturbed on any account. One of them smirked knowingly as he left; I was beyond shame, however, and the Duke was young and good-looking. I had nothing to regret.

I heard nothing from the Duke for the next month. The days passed in the usual mindless round of prayers, meditation, preaching and good works. The Abbess was cautious at first, but, as time passed and the Duke seemed to have forgotten me, she grew bolder and renewed her campaign against me. I was given the most menial and degrading tasks, which I carried out without complaint, yet my acquiescence seemed to infuriate her further instead of pacifying her. She lectured me constantly: I had to learn the virtues of patience and humility, I had to tread my sinful pride underfoot, I had to forsake the lusts of the flesh that had led me to bring shame on my worthy father and that good, good man my would-be husband. To amuse myself in the lonely hours when I was shut up in my cell, with nothing to do except read my Bible and contemplate my unworthiness, I copied down her words, exaggerating and embellishing them, squirming and writhing in self-inflicted reproach and simulated piety till they seemed to me totally ludicrous and I laughed out loud as I reread them.

Then one day I was summoned to visit the Abbess in her study. Her pet lapdog, whom she feeds with choice morsels of venison and cake dipped in wine while the rest of us fast and do penance, rushed at me, snarling and yapping at my ankles; I aimed a kick at it and sent it scurrying for safety underneath a chair where it poked out its ugly snout and growled feebly. The Abbess glared at me, but she had more important things on her mind than to scold me for a minor transgression such as this.

"The Duke will be here tomorrow," she began, "and has particularly asked to see you." She held up her hand to silence me, though I had made no move to speak. "Why he should favour you in this way, I have no idea, but I warn you not to attempt to exploit his interest in you." She droned on about my sinfulness and unhealthy pride, while my heart leapt and I imagined myself set free to paint, to cover the walls of the church with the images that had been churning restlessly in my mind for weeks. At the same time, I strove to keep my excitement under control lest this should be a false alarm: Maybe all he wanted was to sleep with me again, and he would keep tantalising me with the hope of being allowed to paint until he had tired of me. I realised that the Abbess had stopped droning and was looking at me expectantly. "Yes," I assured her, "most certainly, anything you say." She scowled at me suspiciously, told me to remember what she had said and dismissed me.

The Duke arrived the next morning and the day was taken up with the usual activities—hunting, feasting, consultation with the Bishop and the Mayor and other dignitaries—to none of which, of course, I was invited. I heard that the visit was to conclude the following morning with the ceremonial impalement of a dozen or so bandits and robbers, including a woman and a boy of twelve, who had been rounded up over the past few weeks. I waited impatiently till evening and finally, at nine o'clock, the summons came for me.

He was waiting for me alone, having already dismissed the guards; fruit and wine and sweetmeats stood ready on a table beside the bed. He wasted no time on prefatory matters, however, and it was only half an hour later, relaxing beside him, propped up against a silken pillow—so different from the canvas bag full of prickly straw on which I lay my head each night—that I was able to taste them.

"What will the Abbess have to say about this?" I mused, as I popped a grape into my mouth.

"Never mind the Abbess. She'll do as she's told. And so will everyone else. I've informed them that you're to be given every facility to paint and you can start whenever you like."

I was so overjoyed that I threw my arms around his neck and hugged him with genuine fervour. "Only be careful," he went on, disengaging himself and holding me at arm's length, staring seriously into my eyes. "Don't set out deliberately to out-rage them. I can protect you from some things, but not blas-phemy. Just remember that." I promised to take care.

Almost the whole town gathered at the execution field at eight o'clock the next morning. The stakes had already been set in place and the condemned were led towards them joined together in procession by ropes looped around their necks. It was a lovely day—warm, calm and still, with skylarks singing exultantly in the intense blue of the sky. Some of the men looked dazed at the thought of what was about to happen to them: They wept, moaned, prayed, a few begged futilely for mercy from the bystanders, protesting their innocence. Others put on a show of bravado, swaggering with heads held high and bold looks on their faces. Only the child seemed not to understand: He looked around him expectantly and with curiosity; then, when he saw the stakes, he seemed suddenly to realise what was going on and began to cry.

A woman beside me said how sad it was, a youngster like that, couldn't they have let him off? Don't you believe her, a man interrupted, he was the worst of the lot, that brat, despite his air of innocence, a cold-blooded thief and murderer. They discussed this for a moment, then fell silent as the victims gath-ered in the centre of the circle of stakes and received the final rites from the priest. The executioners grabbed the first one and hustled him off. I averted my eyes. I heard a terrible scream and forced myself to look round again: The man was wriggling helplessly with the point of the stake protruding through his belly and out of his back, scrabbling futilely at his body with his hands and kicking his feet. I made myself watch as they took the next one, raised him and brought him down violent-ly on the sharpened wood. In some countries, I had heard, they did it differently, laying the criminal on the ground and bringing the stake down on top of him, pinning him to the earth. Our way, I gathered, was more spectacular and made a more lasting impression on the crowd.

The next man tried to run, but was quickly caught and dragged struggling to his fate, screaming and cursing. I felt I was going to be sick, but continued to look. The lucky ones died almost instantly, from the shock or by having some vital organ pierced right away; one indeed seemed to have died of fright beforehand, for he made no sound at all. Others lingered on, moaning and begging to be released from their misery, but it was forbidden to help them for at least an hour; after that friends and relatives were allowed to finish them off, usually by strangulation or slitting their throats. They left the child till last, presumably because he was lighter and would take less effort; this time I covered my eyes and ears.

When it was over, the audience was allowed to approach the victims, either to comfort them (which was rare) or to mock and torment and revile them in their last moments—for many of those present had suffered from their depredations. I made myself join them, for an idea had occurred to me. I had told the Duke that I would need models for my painting and he had agreed to provide them; but for every Resurrection there is a Crucifixion, for every soul in bliss in paradise another suffering eternal torment in hell. The agony on these faces was real and far beyond anything I could imagine for myself. I studied them for a moment, then hurried off back to the convent to collect some paper and charcoal.

Two

Dorothy was reluctant to recount her morning's reading to Roger, remembering his outburst in the church. When he insisted on knowing, however, she briefly summarised the main points over lunch.

"I told you that woman was sick," he announced triumphantly. "How could she *do* something like that?"

"Something like what? She didn't kill anyone; the authorities did that. She just used the results for her art. Lots of painters have done that, working from the bodies of criminals, even dissecting corpses. You can't always afford to be squeamish."

"But to go and watch it."

"I expect she was forced to, good for her soul or something like that. At any rate she didn't seem to enjoy it, probably unlike most of the rest of the audience. Public executions were one of the main sources of entertainment in her time; I bet they still would be if it were allowed. There's lots of talk now about putting them on television: The ratings would be spectacular."

He decided to change tack. "I don't think much of the way in which she got permission to paint. Smacks of the casting couch to me."

"Why are you so hostile towards her? What else do you expect her to do? She didn't have much choice. It was either do what he wanted or never paint at all and spend the rest of her life in misery and frustration."

"What about that colleague of yours, then, the one you're always complaining about, who got her job by sleeping with the right people?"

"Person. That's different. She *had* a choice, she could have gone elsewhere or she could just possibly have got where she is on ability alone. But she never tried that."

He gave up: It was impossible to argue with her when she was in this mood. "You don't seem to have got very far yet, just a few pages."

"I know. I really don't know how much I'll get through in the time I've got. It's very difficult. First Luigi has to search for the passages he thinks will interest me and then we have to try to decipher her handwriting. It's almost as if she deliberately made the most personal sections particularly difficult to read; maybe that's why they've been largely ignored up till now. The moralising and sermonising—if that's what they really are—present no problem. I doubt if she meant any of that seriously, however."

"You're working on it together, then?"

"Yes."

Side by side, he thought, shoulder to shoulder.

"What about you? I hope you're not getting too bored?"

"Oh, I did some work this morning. I thought I might take the car this afternoon and drive around the lake."

"That could be dangerous, couldn't it?"

"I don't see why. We didn't have any trouble getting here."

"There were U.N. roadblocks every five miles."

"If you're worried, I could take Eva with me. She'd know of any trouble spots."

"Ah. Eva."

"In fact, I'd sort of suggested it to her yesterday. If she was free."

"And of course she is."

"I think so."

"Go ahead, then. Enjoy yourself. I'll see you this evening."

He felt vaguely dissatisfied with her response. What did she expect him to do, all on his own like this? "By the way," he remembered, "that pest Adam was after me again. He's quite determined to get an interview out of you. I said to try around six o'clock. You'd probably better talk to him, otherwise we'll never be rid of him."

"All right. See you at six."

They agreed that he should drive while Eva provided directions. Almost her first act was to pull out a packet of cigarettes and offer him one; he accepted it gratefully. "It's nice not to feel like a criminal for once," he told her. Almost everyone here smoked, he had noticed, apparently incessantly. "Does Luigi?" he asked. "Smoke?"

"Sometimes. Not as much as me."

He thought of Dorothy and Luigi in some stuffy room, studying manuscripts, with Luigi puffing away on the cheap local cigarettes; would she get high-minded, as she did with him, and insist on forbidding it? He would have to ask.

They were quickly out of the town and driving beside the lake; the road at this point came very close to the foot of the mountains. He asked how long she had known Luigi.

"About three months. But it's not all that serious, though he would like it to be."

He tried to study her unobtrusively as he drove. Occasionally she caught his glance and smiled at him, acknowledging his interest. He began to relax and to feel free of the tensions that had been building up—over the past few weeks, as he now admitted, though especially since their arrival. He felt that he could treat Eva as a woman, without having to watch every word and gesture to avoid causing unintentional offence. She leaned back in the seat, stretching out her long, slim legs, with her hands behind her head. Her face was thin and pointed, attractively studded with freckles, the eyes blue, the reddish hair a mass of curls that looked casual but were, he sensed, the product of high art. At first sight she appeared not to use makeup, but here too, he realised, art was concealing art. Dorothy never wore makeup of any kind and, on the whole, he approved, though he would have welcomed some response to his occasional hints that a touch of lipstick might not be out of place now and then. Eva's short skirt rode up as she leaned further back, offering a glimpse of thigh, and the top button of her blouse was undone, revealing that the freckles extended tantalizingly far into her cleavage. Though he knew little about clothes, he could tell that hers were unobtrusively expensive. Dorothy, to be fair, always dressed well too, but for herself rather than for him.

She asked how long he had been married and if they had children.

Three years, he told her. He had been married before and divorced. No children. None with Dorothy either, though not by his decision. He hesitated, wondering if it would be disloyal to tell her more, but it seemed so easy to talk to her that he continued. Dorothy too had been married, with a child, a girl. The girl had been killed in a car accident, at the age of five. The husband had been driving her back from a friend's house and had had "a drink or two" before leaving; he had escaped unhurt. Though no charges were brought against him, Dorothy had blamed him for what happened; they had divorced a few months later. She now said it would hurt too much to have another child.

"I had thought it would help her to forget," he said, "to get over it, but she doesn't see it that way."

Eva showed proper sympathy, that somehow seemed directed more at him than at Dorothy. Some women were like that, she said; they couldn't forget the past and live for the present.

"Like you?"

"Like me." She smiled at him again. She was surprised that Dorothy had not made her feelings clear to him before they were married.

He tried to be fair once again: She *had* told him, but he had thought she would feel different later on.

"She sounds rather selfish to me, especially when it seems to mean so much to you. And rather unreasonable, if her husband really wasn't to blame for the accident. But it's probably not any of my business."

No, it's not, he thought, and I shouldn't be talking to you like this. They were now on the opposite side of the lake, where the landscape was flatter, dotted with fields and clumps of trees, then rising gently to a lower range of mountains. "It looks so peaceful," he said.

"Not when you get close to it." Almost every building had been damaged in the fighting, and most of the fields were overgrown and untended. Many of the farmers had fled and had not yet returned.

"It must have been terrible during the siege?"

She didn't really want to talk about it, it was too horrible to remember. There had been days when bodies lay rotting in the streets because it was too dangerous to venture out and retrieve them. People screaming for help as they lay slowly dying, and no one dared come near them for fear of snipers. People shot down as they tried to leave the town, though you would think the attackers would have welcomed this. Days of near-starvation, with people forced to eat grass, leaves, dogs and rats. She had been lucky, her mother kept some chickens and grew vegetables, they had never had to descend quite to that. It was impossible to catch fish in the lake, even at night; the terrorists used searchlights and had special laser beams on their rifles that could spot targets in the dark. People were dying in the hospital because there were no drugs or medicine, not even bandages, the children whimpering monotonously with pain and no way to help them. Amputations and other operations were performed without anesthetics. She shuddered, thinking about it. She had seen it at firsthand, for she had worked there as a nurse, a volunteer, even though she had no training.

He looked at her with new respect. It was hard to imagine this poised, charming, elegant woman having gone through all this. "Do you think it will start up again?" he asked.

"Probably. Why should it ever end? It's been going on for centuries one way or another."

They stopped at what she said was one of the finest views in the area, looking back at the town across the lake, with the wooded mountains rising behind it. She asked what else he had done since they arrived, and he told her about the frescoes and Adam and the torture museum. She knew Adam by name and had read some of his reports, but had never met him. She had visited the museum once, when she was a teenager, out of morbid curiosity, and had found it revolting. She had never seen the frescoes.

He wondered why not, considering that Luigi—

She hadn't much interest in art, she said, and, from what she had heard, they were the usual religious subjects—saints and miracles and crucifixions—that didn't have much relevance today.

Even if they were by a woman? he hinted.

What difference did that make?

He began to tell her, then realised that he was quoting Dorothy and stopped. They stood side by side, leaning against the car. He wondered what would happen if he touched her hand, but there was no point in making things complicated. A gust of wind blew across the lake, rippling the water. She shivered. "I'm cold," she said. "Let's go back."

He sighed aloud on seeing Adam sitting in the foyer already: It was only five o'clock.

"She's not here yet," he announced curtly. "I thought we'd arranged it for six."

"Yes, I know. I came early because I want to show you something."

"I'm not going back to that museum."

"It's all right. This time it is in my office."

Roger hesitated. "OK. Just give me time to wash and clean up."

"In the meantime I will have a brandy. My paper will pay."

He was relieved to see that there had been no attempt to put back the photograph, though the empty space loomed bare and accusatory. There was nothing he could put in its place, for it had been the only decoration in the otherwise empty, uninviting room. Perhaps Dorothy could turn on the charm and get hold of something else; she was good at that, when she tried. And at so much else. It had been stupid to even think of something with Eva, he realised. Dorothy and he were still happy enough and once she had got over her obsession with these frescoes, things would return to normal.

He refused the offer of a brandy and they set off for Adam's office. "What is it you want to show me?"

Adam said he had been thinking about the photograph that Roger had shown him and his curiosity about what had really happened. Judging by appearance of the men involved, it must have taken place about twenty years ago. He had gone through some of the files of his newspaper and, though he had not come across this particular incident, he had found reports of many similar occurrences. He could translate some of them for Roger, if he wanted.

They were just entering his office as he said this. Roger stopped on the threshold and stared at him. "Why on earth should I want you to do that? And don't you have anything better to do with your time?"

"Sit down, please. I can tell you are excited."

"I'm not excited, just angry. What makes you think I'm interested in this stuff?"

"I can tell you are, though you pretend not to be. Yesterday, at the museum, your voice said no, yet everything else about you said yes. You wanted to stay, to look, but your concern for appearance, for respectability, prevented you. I would not be surprised to find you sneaking back on your own one day, when you thought no one would notice you, like a man ashamed of being seen entering a brothel or a strip show. You know, children are much more honest about this, they flock to the museum at weekends, they cannot get enough of the horrors there, they like to know every little detail."

"You'd think they'd seen enough horrors here in real life."

"Perhaps. Either they succumb to them and become almost catatonic, or they absorb them and learn to live with them and to enjoy them."

"*Enjoy* them?"

"Ignore them, then, treat them as part of normal existence."

He went over to his desk, where a large volume of past issues of the newspaper lay open. "You will find this interesting, I believe. It is a description of a traditional method of killing here called 'The Necktie'; it was very popular twenty years ago. After various kinds of mutilation, depending on whether the victim is male or female, the throat is slit and the tongue pulled out through the gap so that it rests on the chest. A very apt title, don't you think?"

When Roger said nothing, he went on blandly: "Although this particular example is not illustrated, there are several photographs in the museum, very graphic ones. I challenge you to go and look at them—or rather, I challenge you *not* to go and look at them."

"I've had enough of this, and of you. Stay away from me, and stay away from my wife. If you come near me again, I won't answer for the consequences."

"So how did you make out with the gorgeous Eva?"

"All right. We had an interesting drive round the lake."

"And she told you the sad story of her life?"

"Not really. Though she had a pretty tough time here during the siege. She worked as a nurse in the hospital and saw some really dreadful things. I think that says quite a lot for her, especially as she didn't need to do it."

When she made no response to this, he continued, with an edge of anger in his voice, "There's nothing to worry about. She's pleasant company, that's all, and I haven't much else to do."

"There's no need to shout. Do what you like. I just wish she had rather better taste in clothes. She dresses like some cheap harlot."

"What's wrong with her clothes? They seem fine to me." When she again made no response, he decided not to pursue the subject. Her jealousy in this case was irrational, though it had not always been so in the past. He was experiencing a normal response to a particularly attractive woman, that was all.

"How's your Margaret getting on? Still making out with the handsome Duke?"

"We're making better progress now. We've decided to ignore the parts that look easy to read and to concentrate on those that are written in the tiny, cramped handwriting she uses for her personal thoughts and reflections. It's terribly difficult to decipher it, and we have to go on guesswork here and there, but at least we're not wasting time on irrelevant material any longer. I'm still just attempting a very free translation, so it's probably as much my voice as hers a lot of the time, but I find her very congenial somehow, not a figure from the distant past, but someone I would love to meet and chat with. The only problem—for me, at least—is that Luigi smokes all the time, those dreadful, locally produced cigarettes. It's a tiny room, and the air is literally blue after an hour. If it goes on much longer, I'll have to ask him to stop. I tried some discreet coughing, but it had no effect."

He smiled and said nothing. Perhaps her hostility towards

Eva was also tinged by her own interest in Luigi: No doubt she felt that Eva wasn't good enough for him.

"Before we left, we went to pay a courtesy call on his boss. It was like something out of the 1890s—this huge, fat monster of a man, still in his dressing gown, sprawled all over a sofa, the air thick with perfume and incense, a box of chocolates and a bottle of liqueur within easy reach, a scratchy record of an aria from *Tosca* on the gramophone. He held up his hand with a lordly gesture to keep us silent till it had finished."

"This was in his *office?*"

"That's what Luigi called it, but really it's also his study. He has an apartment in the museum. He was very gracious, kissed my hand—without getting up, I almost had to kneel—welcomed me to his unhappy country, bemoaned the barbarous nature of the times, flirted with me in an elephantine sort of way, recommended the fish in the restaurant we've eaten in, assured me that Luigi would attend to my every need—no suggestion that *he* would do anything to help—and politely dismissed us. As we were leaving, he was already putting on another record, *Rigoletto*, I think. No mention whatever of the frescoes. I doubt if he's ever seen them, even though he's nominally responsible for them; it would be too much effort to walk over to the church. He insisted on speaking bad English to me all the time and called me his 'dear lady.'"

She looked at her watch. "Shouldn't that journalist be here by now?"

"No, he's not coming. I told him to stay away."

"Why?"

"He's crazy. He's got it into his head that I have a perverted fascination with all the horrible things that have gone on here. So every time he sees me, he drags me off to look at evidence of some atrocity or other. He did that again this afternoon and I told him I didn't want to have anything more to do with him."

"That's your privilege. It doesn't mean *I* can't see him. I can make up my own mind about that."

"But the man's a lunatic. He described some hideous method of killing to me and then challenged me *not* to go and look at photographs of it in the museum."

"Lunatic or not, I want to meet him. I don't often get the chance to be a celebrity, even if it's for some local rag in the middle of nowhere."

"Do what you want. You'll probably have to go to his office to make an appointment, though. I think I've scared him off from here for good."

But he hadn't. When they went downstairs, Adam was sitting in the foyer waiting for them. He stood up as they entered, smiled nervously at Roger, took off his hat and bowed to Dorothy, and replaced his hat on his head.

Roger gave a snort of disgust. "If you insist on this, I don't suppose there's anything I can do to stop you. I'll see you at the restaurant. I told Eva we'd be there by seven. It seems to be the only decent place to eat and she said they were going there anyway."

"What an amazing coincidence. I made exactly the same arrangement with Luigi."

Adam relaxed a little once Roger had left. "Let me offer you a brandy," he suggested, ushering her into the bar. "My paper will pay."

She accepted and sat down facing him across a small table. "I apologise for my husband. There seems to be some misunderstanding between you."

"No misunderstanding, I assure you. He is just unwilling to

look hard at the truth. I would rather we spoke English, if you don't mind. It will be good practice for me."

He began with some routine questions about her background and seemed surprised to learn that this was actually her birthplace. She thought it strange that Roger had failed to mention this, even if he had seemed more concerned with misleading Adam than with enlightening him.

"Yes," she said, "I lived here till I was five, though I don't remember it very well. Just the house and the orchard inside a walled garden and my brother, whom I used to play with. I don't remember any other friends; I was a rather lonely child. And we used to go for picnics on the weekends in the hills and my father would take me out rowing on the lake. That was before the war started up again and we had to leave—we were the wrong class, the wrong nationality, the wrong religion, the wrong everything. My parents never came back."

He asked how she had come to learn about the frescoes, scribbling the answers in pencil, with his pad propped unsteadily on his knee rather than on the table. When she admitted that she was not the famous academic superstar that Roger had made her out to be, he laughed and said he had never really believed that: Her husband was not very skilled at lying.

"No, he's not," she agreed thoughtfully. "But he thinks he is."

He had clearly examined the frescoes carefully and asked intelligent questions about them. "And what do you think of Margaret herself? What impression do you have of her as a person?"

"It's too early to say yet; I'll have to read more of her journals before I decide. So far, I find her attractive—independent, outspoken, talented, spiritually liberated, yet oppressed by the male-dominated society of her time—a true feminist heroine. It's almost too perfect, I'm afraid."

"Why do you say that? Are you not a feminist yourself?"

"Yes and no. To the extent that any thinking woman is nowadays, yes. But not to the extent that my husband seems to believe I am."

"He is frightened for you?"

"If you mean *of* me, yes, I think he is sometimes, certainly recently. But this has nothing to do with Margaret or the frescoes."

"Of course not. I apologise."

He offered her another brandy, which she refused—"Even if your paper is paying." He gave an embarrassed smile. "It is one of the few—how do you say it, perks?—available to me in my job. Actually, to tell the truth, my editor does not always pay, not unless he likes what I write. But it helps people to relax, to talk."

Before leaving, he asked if she intended to visit the caves.

"What caves?"

"Surely you know about them? Where Margaret spent the last few years of her life. After she was banished from the convent."

"No, I hadn't heard about that."

"Ask your friend Luigi, the curator. And it is in all the guidebooks. I would tell you more about it now, but I have to leave for an appointment—perhaps some other time. Although it might be too dangerous to visit them now in any event, with the bandits still there in the hills."

She tried to find out more, but he insisted that he had to leave. "Here is my card. You can phone me or leave a message. It is an interesting story."

But when she asked Luigi about this at dinner, he was brusquely dismissive. "A legend," he assured her. "There is no evidence for it whatsoever."

"But he said it was in all the guidebooks."

"You don't think that proves anything, do you? All guide-books are filled with rumours and exotic folktales."

"Well, what *is* the rumour then?"

"Briefly, that after she was stopped from completing her work on the frescoes and they were walled over, she was exiled to some caves in the mountains. The earliest monks had lived in them, before they built the monastery and the convent in the town, under conditions of great hardship and isolation. The Duke had died, killed in some foreign war, and she no longer had a protector, so it was easy to get rid of her. She was made to live in a cave that was accessible only by a rope ladder—which they took away once she was inside. Once a week they supplied her with provisions that were put in a basket and drawn up by some kind of pulley. She lived there for five years, or ten, or twenty, or fifty, whichever version you want to believe."

"How horrible."

"*If* you believe the story, yes. The truth appears to be that she died peacefully in her bed in the convent at the ripe old age of seventy-five. Oh—and it's said that she painted her last great masterpiece there, inside the cave. No one has even actually *seen* it, because no one knows any longer which of several dozen caves she is supposed to have lived in, and they are all far too difficult to get to anyway, and no one has explained where she got the paint and other materials from, especially when it was her painting that got her into trouble in the first place—but you don't look for consistency in a myth, do you?"

"Speak English," Roger interrupted, staring at them distrustfully. She wondered why he bothered even to be jealous, after gazing soulfully into Eva's eyes all evening, hardly touching his food, hanging on her every word. Did Luigi notice this too, and did he care? He appeared not to, but perhaps he was just being polite.

• • •

"What are you reading?"

"A guidebook. The one I found a couple of nights ago. I want to see if it says anything about the caves."

"What caves?"

"Where Margaret is reputed to have spent her last years. Luigi and I were talking about them at dinner. When you got all hot and bothered and barged in."

"It's irritating when you jabber away to him all the time in a language I can't understand."

"I'm surprised you even noticed, you were so wrapped up with Eva."

"Well, at least she talks to me."

"So would Luigi, if you gave him the chance. But you've loftily ignored him ever since you met."

"I don't like the way he's always fawning over you."

"And I don't like the way you're always fawning over Eva, so that makes us even, doesn't it? Look," she went on after a pause, "let's not quarrel about this. Not here. Not now. My relations with Luigi are purely business: He's nice and helpful and I like him. My main priority at the moment is to find out as much as I can about Margaret and her work in the short time I have available. I can't afford to waste time on jealousy and suspicion—on either side. If you're bored here and feel you would rather be at home, then leave. I'll be back in two or three weeks."

Leaving you here with Luigi, he thought, knowing that she knew he thought it. "I'll think about it. Meanwhile I want to go to sleep. Don't keep the light on too long."

Despite the light, he was asleep almost immediately, and snoring. The guidebook, once she had struggled through its losing battle with the English language, offered some interesting, if suspect, information: Margaret was the reputed creator of a scandalous series of frescoes painted under the patronage of Duke Alexander the Bold, later destroyed or at least lost. The centrepiece had been a blasphemous (a term the book forbore to elaborate on) vision of hell, and many of the other paintings offered graphic depictions of murder, torture and dismemberment—acceptable enough at the time except that they had, allegedly, been painted from life, for Margaret was supposed to have persuaded the Duke (who was known to be her lover) to put condemned criminals to death in various ingenious and cruel ways in order to be able to depict their sufferings in her painting. She was also rumoured to have had a daughter by the Duke, whose fate was unknown, though she was commonly believed to have been murdered—probably by Margaret herself. Finally, on the Duke's death, the indignant population demanded her expulsion from the convent and the destruction of her paintings; she was banished to a remote cave in the mountains where she languished for several years, crazed by grief and belated remorse. On her death, she was found to have been working on a final painting, a paradise to set against her hell, using ashes mixed with her own blood as her paint, and twigs, pieces of burnt stick and her fingers instead of brushes.

It was certainly ingenious, Dorothy thought, based on a mixture of half-truths and the normal prejudice directed against anyone who stepped out of line in any rigidly conformist society. As she was also a woman, she would, of course, have to be credited with sexual crimes as well, especially infanticide. She wondered about the painting of hell, though: Had that ever really existed except in the lurid imaginations of Margaret's enemies? Had it really been destroyed, or was it still waiting to be discovered, walled up as the other paintings had been, but not yet brought to light? The "paradise" could surely be discounted, however. If there was any truth to the story, it was probably based on frenzied and despairing daubings made by a woman driven beyond the point of endurance, scraping her hands against the stone walls until the blood ran. Nevertheless she would ask Luigi about it again tomorrow.

✠✠✠ Margaret ✠✠✠

I was anxious to begin right away, but of course there were endless preliminaries to go through first—obtaining supplies, scaffolding, above all preparing the walls to receive the paint. I had no idea how to set about this and had never painted a fresco before, but I had asked the Duke to provide me with some writings on the subject and was determined to try. I felt vaguely that if they didn't like the results—and I was pretty sure that they wouldn't—it would be easier for them to destroy individual canvases than the whole wall of a building. And if I mixed things up a bit—something conventionally orthodox and impeccably pious alongside the kind of image that was buzzing around in my head all night and keeping me from sleeping—then it would make removal even more difficult.

Again, I had mentioned some of this to the Duke and he had promised to send some craftsmen and workmen to assist, but once more days and weeks dragged by and nothing happened. The Abbess took heart at this. She assumed that the Duke had had his fun, made the kind of promises men always do in these situations and forgotten all about me, while I, poor, naive, innocent child—she actually called me that one day when she had imbibed rather too much wine and was feeling unnaturally sentimental—had made the mistake of believing every word he said. She was more shocked, it seemed, at the idea of my

painting the church than at my having been, however briefly, the Duke's mistress: The latter, however regrettable, especially for a nun, was the normal fate of any woman, while the former was not merely unladylike but positively immoral. It was just as well, she said, that I would never get the chance after all, but, to be on the safe side, she refrained from making life too hard for me, so that if the Duke *did* make good on his word, I would have nothing to complain of regarding her.

As time lay heavily on my hands as a result, I thought I would at least begin to make some preliminary sketches, and reminded the Abbess that the Duke had promised that I could use some of my fellow nuns, and even some of the monks, as models. She put up a struggle here—monks, she said, were totally out of the question until she received specific instructions in writing from the Duke, but I *could* use a few of the nuns if any of them were willing to degrade themselves in this way, which she very much doubted. In the event, once the news got round, I had to fight them off. Anything was better, it seemed, than spending hours kneeling in endless prayer or penance on a cold stone floor, washing dishes or churning butter.

I chose two or three with particularly striking features and used them for the women handling the body in a descent from the cross. I had the face of Christ already from one of the men who had been impaled but, when they saw the results, my models were outraged. How could I perform such sacrilege, using the face of a common criminal to represent our Lord? It was indecent to portray him in this way, with protruding tongue, staring eyes and gaping mouth. His features must be calm and serene, showing his ultimate victory over death and Satan. Yes, he must have suffered, but the point was to show the transcendence, not the pain; the achievement, not the defeat. My drawing was ugly, immoral, evil and they had no wish to be associated with it. I should tear it up at once before anyone else could see it and be contaminated by it.

I tried to point out that crucifixion *was* a hideously painful and lingering death, even worse than impaling, which was merciful by comparison. This—or something like it—was how a crucified person *would* look. Why attempt to conceal it or deny it? It was no use, however. Either I destroyed the drawing or I lost their services and their goodwill. I remembered the Duke's advice—don't set out deliberately to outrage them—and thought it best to compromise, at least for the moment. I tore the drawing up.

After a few days' contemplation, I decided on a different approach: This time I would work on a Raphael-style Virgin and child, full of sweetness and light, with nothing in it that could possibly offend. I sent out a request for models and, after rejecting (not without a certain satisfaction) those who had objected to my previous effort, chose a certain Angelica, a young woman whose calm and serene features—not to mention her name—stood in marked contrast to the sordid stories whispered about her earlier career, which had led to her being bundled off into the convent for much the same reasons as I had but on an infinitely larger and more exotic scale.

And at once the protests started: I had hardly begun my first sketch when I received an official delegation headed by Sister Maria, a woman of indeterminate age whose own credentials with regard to virginity were certainly impeccable. She seemed to assume that her name and status should have entitled her to play the central role in my painting; at any rate she objected vigorously (backed up by those who accompanied her) to my employing a "cheap harlot" whose virginity had probably departed in her cradle.

It was what Angelica *looked like* that mattered, I explained patiently, not what she *was*. She had the ideal presence for the Virgin and radiated an almost palpable sense of purity. What did it matter if that was not her true personality? If the image I created inspired devotion and worship from those who contemplated it, then I had succeeded in capturing an inner, permanent truth that was far more significant than the "truths" of external character and behaviour.

No, Sister Maria said firmly. If the soul is corrupt and rotten, then this will show in the features, however much you may try to disguise it. Inner and external truth must be in harmony if the image is to achieve its task of enlightening the spirit and leading it towards a wise understanding of the divine purpose.

Maybe, I replied, but, by your logic, only the Virgin herself could pose for a portrait of the Virgin. No one else could possibly be perfect enough. It makes the task of the painter impossible.

Then perhaps it should be. Perhaps it is blasphemy for one to attempt to use the merely human as a means of portraying the divine. For lesser subjects, yes, but not for this one.

Possibly I was wrong about her, I thought, and she was not simply jealous of Angelica. She seemed dreadfully sincere, and there is no answer the artist can make to wrongheaded and passionate sincerity. I thought of someone who had visited us while I still lived at home and enjoyed my father's favour; he had visited Kiev and Muscovy and Novgorod and spoke about the holy icons he had seen there, marvelling especially over those by someone I had never heard of, a monk called Andrei Roublev. What characterised these icons, he said, was the complete fusion of the human and the divine, the spiritual and the material: Christ was literally *in* the icon that portrayed him, and the image was a direct and palpable link between the worshipper and that which was worshipped. Perhaps, in her own bungling way, that was what Sister Maria was talking of too.

All right, I conceded, I won't use Angelica as a model for the Virgin; in fact, I won't use any model at all. But will you at least permit me to use my imagination instead?

She proved unexpectedly magnanimous in victory. I could use a model after all, she conceded graciously, provided that her moral stature was impeccable and, to my dismay, she pushed forward someone who had been hovering behind her, a fat, half-witted, middle-aged woman who had been dumped in the convent by her family at the age of about ten and had spent the rest of her life there. Use Sister Helena, she ordered, and turned on her heel and swept off, followed by the rest of her acolytes.

I told Angelica—who had listened impassively to the stream of imputations on her moral character—that she would no longer be needed, and she flounced off, muttering that she was bored out of her mind already and didn't see the point of painting yet another Virgin anyway: There were too many of them around as it was. Helena beamed at me expectantly; she was always smiling and it was impossible to know if she had understood anything of what had been going on. I asked her to take Angelica's place and to hold the bundle of cloth that was doing service for the infant Christ. What would Sister Maria have said, I wondered, if I had insisted on using a real baby too, and where would we have obtained one?

The Siege

. . .

In the event, things worked out surprisingly well. Helena was far from beautiful, yet she radiated an uncomplicated goodness and kindness that seemed to suit the nature of the Virgin far better than any conventional prettiness. I made no attempt to flatter her and drew her just as she was—the double chin, the puffy cheeks, the squint, the thinning hair—and yet the result *was* beautiful and seemed to me to say more about motherhood than anything I could have achieved with Angelica. I showed the drawing to the Abbess and a few of the nuns like Sister Maria with a good deal of trepidation. Some, as I had expected, hated it and found it ugly, disrespectful and even (the usual complaint) blasphemous; others were surprisingly complimentary. Maria, to my amazement, approved of it. I could have softened some of the features, she observed, and eliminated the squint and the wart on the right cheek, but the woman's inner goodness shone through the outward imperfections and redeemed them. I had captured both human and divine love in a way, she conceded, that was remarkable. The Abbess was noncommittal. She had come, it was obvious, prepared to carp and find fault, but she also looked to Maria for her aesthetic judgements and was somewhat taken aback by her mentor's unexpected praise. It was good enough, she mumbled, if you like that kind of thing, but personally she preferred something more elevated and uplifting.

And then, after all the delays, things suddenly began to move with what seemed lightning speed. Workmen turned up one day without warning and demanded detailed instructions as to what they were supposed to do. Fortunately, I had made some preliminary plans and was able to get them started on some minor tasks while I asked to speak to the master craftsman about preparing the wall so that it would receive and hold the paint. He tried to wave me away at first, saying that it was a man's job and he would look after it, but I persisted, insisting that it was of the utmost importance to me to know exactly what I was doing, and why. He then attempted to fob me off with explanations that would barely have challenged the intelligence of a child, and it was only when I threatened him with the Duke's most severe displeasure that he grudgingly agreed to take me seriously. Once he realised, however, that I *did* know something about what I was doing and I was not just some spoiled and privileged young lady trying to evade the tedium of convent life, he relaxed considerably and we became good friends, and spent several happy hours going into every detail of just how to prepare and maintain the surface and exactly how to mix the paints so that they would not dry and flake off or fade into invisibility after a couple of years.

As it all now began to look rather more complicated than I had expected, I reminded the Abbess that I would need an assistant and that this would have to be a man as there was heavy work to be done, especially in moving scaffolding about. I had already written to the Duke, I said, forestalling her objection, and had received his permission for this; he also authorised me to use monks as models if necessary. She read the letter with furrowed brows and a scowl on her face, though she had no alternative but to acquiesce. She would not be responsible, she informed me darkly, for anything that happened to me under the circumstances; she hereby withdrew her protection and, if rape and other unspeakable violations resulted, I had only myself to blame. She said this in a tone that suggested she would be more than gratified if something of this kind actually happened, for it would teach me a well-deserved lesson. I replied that I was prepared to take the risk but was certain that the sanctity of the church and my nun's cowl and habit would secure me from all harm.

The assistant assigned to me is a monk called Dimitrios, who claims to be of Greek origin and to have spent his childhood and early manhood in at least a dozen different countries, including China and the Indies, before ending up here. I can't quite make out yet whether he is simpleminded or just rather strange in his manner of thinking. He does everything he is told to do willingly and efficiently, but his conversation is often extremely bizarre. Yesterday, for instance, was a swelteringly hot day and I was under siege from flies buzzing around my head and constantly settling on any exposed skin. I was swatting ineffectually at them, with increasing irritation, and cursing under my breath, when he gently reprimanded me. They are God's creatures too, he told me, and equally deserving of enjoying life. With all due respect, I responded, he seems to have made a bad mistake here and I would certainly be very happy if they would go and enjoy it somewhere else, preferably on another planet.

Not so, he assured me, for they are necessary scavengers and cleansers: The world would be heaped knee-high with dung, for example, if flies did not exist.

(Me): "Then they should mind their own business and stay away from humans."

(Him): "But they love men and wish to help them."

(Me): "How so?"

(Him): "That fly buzzing around your head is trying to communicate with you, even if you do not know this. Why do you think he follows you everywhere? If you walk down the corridor, he will go with you; if you open a door or a window to set him free, he will refuse to leave."

(Me): "That's because they're stupid. A fly can get *into* a room through a crack in a window half an inch wide, but it can't get out again even if you throw the window wide open."

(Him): "Because he does not *want* to leave."

I gave up: "So what is this particular fly trying to tell me, then?"

"That, I don't know. One day, perhaps, we will learn to communicate with them and share their wisdom. They have been around much longer than we have and will certainly outlast us."

That notion, I observed, bordered on heresy. "Surely when *we* go, everything else goes too?"

"Not necessarily. God created the world in seven days, and insects, you will remember, preceded man. Why should not the reverse process take place on the Day of Judgement: Mankind's destiny is concluded first, but the beasts and the fish and the birds and the insects survive him—for a time."

"Two or three days, perhaps."

"That all depends on how you define a biblical 'day.' Some of the church fathers have argued that it might represent a period of weeks or even years. It is quite possible that flies may survive man, then, for as much as one hundred years."

I give this conversation in detail as one of the oddest that we have had so far, but there have been others equally strange.

THREE

She showed Luigi the guidebook, but he remained unimpressed: "The usual kind of scandal and innuendo surrounding anyone—especially, in this context, a woman—who dared to live and behave in an unconventional way. There is no real evidence for any of it."

"Except for the paintings themselves. And a year ago, you would have denied *their* existence."

"That's true. All right, we know from her journal that she used the bodies and faces of executed criminals as models for her pictures. That gets exaggerated by her enemies into the claim that she had them deliberately tortured and killed for this purpose. Do you know the films of Tarkovsky, the Russian director?"

"Yes, I've seen *The Sacrifice*. That's his, isn't it? But what's that got to do with it?"

"In his diary he mentions that while he was shooting another film, *Solaris*, his enemies in the cultural bureaucracy—this was in the Brezhnev era when anything unconventional was frowned on—claimed that he had arranged for a condemned criminal to be executed in front of the cameras to make a particular scene more authentic. It was all ridiculous, of course, and no such scene even exists in the film, but there you have an example of a similar kind of malicious rumour from today."

"Didn't he make a film about Andrei Roublev too? Margaret mentions him."

"Yes. I'm sure you've seen Roublev's *Trinity*, at least in reproduction. For Tarkovsky he was the antithesis of the other painters of his time, who wanted to frighten people into repentance by showing a vengeful God who tormented sinners and punished them with eternal suffering. Roublev, on the other hand, portrayed a loving and forgiving God."

"Not exactly Margaret's style."

"Her work *does* seem rather bitter and angry, though perhaps you can't blame her, under the circumstances."

"In that case, why couldn't she have painted a hell after all, as the guidebook says? Everything we have is on one single wall of the church; perhaps there are other paintings still hidden on the opposite wall, underneath all that sickly, sentimental nineteenth-century trash?"

"What do you expect me to do? Knock the wall down, to find out?"

"I don't see what real difference that would make." Her gaze drifted up to the gaping hole in the roof, under which a plastic sheet had been hung to catch rainwater. "A few more chips of plaster on the floor would hardly be noticed among all this rubble. We could knock a few pieces out here and there, to see."

"I don't have authority to do that."

"Ask your boss. Or the priest."

"The priest was killed during the siege and hasn't been

70

replaced yet. There is a home for mentally retarded children here and he was trying to lead them to safety, under a flag of truce. A sniper shot him, very neatly, right in the middle of the forehead. He got a couple of the children too. They were too confused and upset to run for safety."

She was silent for a moment, remembering her brother. The bullet hole in *his* forehead had been far from neat. What kind of pleasure did a person like that get, using children for target practice? Mark fell from the tree once more, quietly, like a stone. With difficulty, she picked up the conversation once more.

"I doubt if your boss would care what we did, would he?"

"Probably not. I'll think about it, though I really don't think we would find anything."

"What do you think about the alleged child, the daughter?" Another image flashed before her—David's ashen face as he struggled to tell her what had happened to Jill. They had refused at the hospital to let her see the body until it had been "tidied up," in case it would distress her too much. As if that made it any easier to bear the loss. Once again she had to struggle to cope with what Luigi was saying.

"That might well be true—that she had one, at any rate, not that she murdered it. But it was also a standard accusation of the time, especially where nuns were concerned. And you can certainly forget about some final masterpiece languishing undiscovered in a cave."

She sighed. "You're doing a good job of destroying all my dreams. Can't you leave me with any illusions?"

"Surely there's enough here with what we've got, the paintings and the journals. But I promise to bring a hammer and chisel with me tomorrow."

Before they parted, she asked if they could put some time aside one evening once they had finished work to look for the house she used to live in. "I've no real idea how to find it," she confessed, "yet something tells me I would recognise it if I saw it."

He would ask among his friends and family, he said, if anyone remembered her parents, but it was a long time since they had lived there, and much had happened in the interval. Alarmed that he had somehow offended her, he blushed and stammered something about how youthful she still looked nonetheless. "It's because I never use makeup," she told him gravely. "The secret of an eternal schoolgirl complexion. Ask Eva about it sometime, she ought to know."

Eva was busy—she had to sell *some* clothes, she told Roger, in order to stay alive—but she would meet him for a coffee in the late afternoon. He felt restless and disoriented and, after trying and failing to do some work, decided to go out and wander round the Old Town. Dorothy had said he could visit her at any time—she spent the mornings in the church, examining the frescoes, and the afternoons poring over the journals—but he had lost all interest in Margaret and her work and had made it clear that he had no desire to listen to any more extracts from her diary. He knew he was being unreasonable and that his deliberately slighting responses to her enthusiastic reports hurt her more than she cared to acknowledge, but he was bored beyond endurance with the whole business. And then, when they got home, she would be the centre of attention at parties, telling everyone about her wonderful discoveries, while he hovered, grey and unnoticed, in the background. . . .

The only thing that was keeping him here, he admitted to himself, was Eva, and that was on the verge of becoming dangerous. He was finding it increasingly difficult to keep his hands off her, especally when, as had happened last night, they sat squeezed close together at dinner and her leg was pressed tightly against his. But this was also, he realised, an argument *for* leaving, before he found himself doing something foolish.

He recognised the street he was in as the one he had walked through on their first evening, when the woman had grabbed at his arm, and looked round warily, as if afraid she might accost him again. Had she been offering sex, or had she just been begging for money? She had seemed, from her clothing, to be a Gypsy; there were a lot of them around, begging on street corners, accompanied by innumerable ragged children, or squatting outside the churches with outstretched hands, wailing monotonously. He had attempted the day before to give money to one particularly pathetic-looking specimen, but Eva had dragged him away. They're all frauds, she assured him, or spies for the terrorists. They've got plenty of money; they drive from one town to another in Mercedeses. He had felt uneasy, nevertheless, partly at what still seemed to him their obvious misery, and partly at her open contempt and hostility. And then later there had been some casually derogatory remark about Jews. . . .

And now he found himself where his footsteps had been leading him all the time, though without conscious intention: outside the museum of torture. That little bastard Adam had been right, Roger thought; perhaps he was skulking around somewhere in the shadows waiting for him, gloating already. "I challenge you *not* to go and look," he had smirked; well, he *would* go anyway, and the hell with Adam. But he would do it openly and boldly, not like a client trying to slither unnoticed into a brothel.

The place seemed empty, with no one except a bored attendant collecting admission money. He would force himself to go round slowly, looking at everything this time, and, yes, he would acknowledge that there was a certain morbid fascination mixed in with the genuine revulsion that he felt. Somewhere in the world, at this very moment, someone was undergoing agonies like those depicted here. Surely it was better to face up to this rather than trying to ignore it? In his own small way he was committed to redressing injustice and trying to protect the weak and helpless, though he was lucky enough to live in a country where something as blatantly vile as all this rarely occurred. Yet it *could* happen, easily enough, even in the most apparently civilised of countries, if the right—or the wrong—people were allowed to seize power.

Though he could not understand the written descriptions, the visual information was usually explicit enough. In the first room, there was a woodcut of a man hanging suspended by a pulley above an oversized cauldron with a lighted fire beneath it; he was being lowered into this feet first while onlookers standing on a platform round the rim of the cauldron watched with interest. Roger knew what this was: a traditional medieval punishment for forgers, who were boiled in oil. In the room with the life-sized reproductions a man was tied to a bench while a goat licked the soles of his bare feet; he had found this comical when he first saw it, but Adam had explained happily that this was one of the most unbearable of torments. The feet were constantly smeared with salt, to keep the goat at work with its rough tongue; gradually the skin and flesh were worn away, down to the bone. Few men—or women—lasted more than an hour or two without going mad.

He was examining one of the photographs when he heard a voice in his ear: "A favourite torture of the Savak, the secret police of the late Shah of Iran, called 'The Frying Pan.' The victim is strapped onto a metal table, which is gradually heated by means of electricity until the pain is unbearable. A well-known ayatollah called Saidi was one of many killed in this way. And then, of course, the ayatollahs themselves came to power and developed their own equally ingenious methods of execution."

It was Adam, of course, smiling at him blandly. Roger felt like hitting him, but quickly controlled his anger. He had been well and truly caught out and Adam had done nothing worse than read his intentions more honestly than he had done himself.

"If you are finished here for the time being," Adam went on, "I will invite you to lunch. And this time *I* will pay." He led the way to a small restaurant nearby, dark and cramped and containing not more than half a dozen tables. The owner obviously recognised him and greeted him effusively. Without consulting Roger, Adam ordered two brandies. "The best food in town is here," he told Roger. "Most people go to the fish restaurant, but it is nothing compared to this." There was no menu; Adam simply asked the owner what he was cooking today, passed on the three possibilities to Roger and ordered for them both.

When the brandy arrived, Adam raised his glass in a toast: "To your wife. She is a very remarkable woman. Talented, intelligent and beautiful. You are a very lucky man."

"Beautiful" was going a bit too far, Roger thought, though Dorothy was certainly still attractive. Especially when she smiled, which she did so rarely now, and her eyes lit up and the full lips parted to reveal her slightly crooked teeth. Yet he would be inclined to call Eva beautiful. He acknowledged the toast nevertheless. "Yes, I am lucky, I suppose."

"You *suppose*? Most men would give their right arm for a woman like that. You must be careful to treat her well."

What business is it of yours? Roger thought. Everyone here seemed to want to pry into his private life. "Are *you* married?" he inquired.

"Alas, no. Though I have had my chances." Adam made no attempt to elaborate on this and, when the food arrived, devoted his full attention to that and said little more. When he had finished, he wiped his mouth with his napkin with great satisfaction and ordered coffee and more brandy. "This one my editor will pay for."

The meal was good, and the brandy and the bottle of wine that had accompanied it were making Roger drowsy. He failed at first to register Adam's next remark and the man had to repeat it.

"Your wife seems very interested in the caves."

"What caves?"

"In the mountains. Where Sister Margaret was banished."

"Oh, her."

"If you like, I can provide you with a guide, someone who is on good terms with the terrorists who lurk there. Otherwise, you might be held for ransom." He chuckled, as if he had made a joke. "They are very dangerous people."

"I don't want to go to any caves. And I don't think my wife does either."

"In that case, I must have made a mistake. The guide is very reliable. You may have met her; she is called Eva and is a friend of the assistant curator of the town museum. Would you care for another brandy?"

Roger ignored the invitation. "You *have* made a mistake," he agreed. "I know Eva and I know that she has nothing to do with the terrorists. She hates them. She worked in the hospital while they were bombarding it. She saw the suffering they caused."

"Nevertheless, she has contacts there. A lover, I believe. But then she has many lovers."

He felt his earlier hostility to the man returning. "I've got to go now," he said, rising to his feet and almost knocking the table over as he pushed it away. "I'll pay for the meal." He pulled a bundle of gaudily coloured bank notes from his pocket and threw them down on the table. "Don't call me," he added, as he stumbled out the door, blinking in the intensity of the sunlight that struck him almost physically, like a blow. "I'll call you."

"You look upset," Eva told him. "Is anything wrong?"

"No, just the heat. And too much to drink at lunchtime." He had gone back to the hotel to lie down and had fallen asleep, waking up with a start and perhaps even a yell with the conviction that something was steadily licking the sole of his foot, scraping nearer and nearer to the bone. But it was just a breeze blowing through the open window and rustling the sheet against his foot. Looking at his watch, he realised that it was past four and he was late for their appointment; he had half-run most of the way, making himself feel even worse.

"Did you eat alone?"

"No, with that little swine Adam. I ran into him"—he was going to say "at the torture museum," but changed that to "in the street."

"You don't like him, do you?"

"Obviously not. He seems to have a knack for bringing out the worst in me, rubbing me the wrong way."

She murmured something sympathetic, but did not ask for further details. He wondered whether to mention the caves, but as he had no intention of going there anyway, it seemed unnecessary to raise the subject. The man was certainly lying in any case.

"Do you like dancing?" she asked suddenly.

"I used to. My first wife, Stephanie, did. But I haven't done it much recently."

"Tell me about her."

"There's not much to say. It was a bad mistake, on both our parts." It had taken less than a year to realise it. At first he had welcomed her unconventionality, her freedom, her vivaciousness, then it had come to irritate and alarm him. He was a young lawyer, struggling to establish himself, and had neither the time nor money to go to parties all the time, or the theatre or to eat out rather than have her cook—she hated cooking, she said, just as she hated all kinds of household slavery. And so, when he was unable to share her enjoyments, she found others to take his place, lots of them. It had all ended in bitterness and acrimony, even hatred—a common enough story.

"And Dorothy is different?"

"She's much more serious, and quieter. And a lot more intelligent. We get on pretty well together. But in some ways she doesn't really—" He was about to say "understand me," but the ludicrousness of the cliché stopped him in time. "We get along all right."

"I don't think she likes me very much."

"To tell you the truth, I think she's a little bit jealous. You *are* a very attractive woman, you know." He considered for a moment placing his hand on hers, which was lying conveniently close on the surface of the table, but restrained himself.

"Thank you, kind sir. And you're a very attractive man. She's probably wise to be jealous."

Not all that attractive, he thought; a little overweight despite his twice-weekly game of squash, thinning hair that was also turning grey—a distinguished grey, Dorothy said. He felt flattered all the same.

"So what's all this about dancing?"

"If you're interested, there's another restaurant that has a band and a dance floor. The food is terrible, but we could eat here as usual and go along there afterwards."

"What about Dorothy and Luigi?"

"They could come too, of course, though Luigi hates dancing. I can never get him to come with me, so I usually go on my own."

"Dorothy likes it. She always says we should do it more often."

"Do what?" She smiled at him knowingly.

"Go dancing, of course. What else would I mean?"

"Well, in that case, I'm sure Luigi will come too."

The band, both Dorothy and Roger quickly realised, was quite appallingly bad: half a dozen balding, overweight men, playing an incongruous assortment of instruments with little enthusiasm and less ability. Their only display of animation came during the regulation pause that followed every fourth number when they were supplied with large mugs of beer that they drank thoughtfully, chatting quietly among themselves. Their repertoire seemed limited to ten numbers, played and repeated in strict rotation. Some were unfamiliar, but about half were barely recognisable as English-language popular songs from the 1960s, usually sung by the trombonist in a monotone that suggested the words had been memorised but not at all understood.

Eva, however, seemed contented enough, humming along with the music and tapping the fingers of her right hand on her knee. Luigi was silent and morose and obviously ill at ease; he sat nursing a glass of Coca-Cola, having refused anything stronger. They had arrived just before the band broke off for refreshments; when it started up again, Roger asked Dorothy to dance, after glancing inquiringly at both Eva and Luigi to see if they wanted to take the initiative.

Though it was a long time since they had danced together, they found their old rhythm easily enough. But it was difficult to manoeuvre on the cramped and tiny floor among the half-dozen other couples, many of whom were drunk and seemed more interested in performing acrobatics than in dancing, so that their bodies came into frequent and painful contact. After two sessions of receiving elbows in her back and ribs and violent kicks on her shins, Dorothy said she had had enough and led the way back to the table.

"What about you?" Roger asked, hovering over Eva. The frenzy of the last number had given way to something slower, almost waltzlike, and the room seemed darker, lit mainly by a large revolving ball of multicoloured glass that sent random shafts of red, green and yellow light over the dance floor. She nodded, stood up and took his hand. He noticed that Dorothy glanced briefly at Luigi, who shook his head.

"Don't bother with him," Eva advised, laughing, "he's clumsier than an elephant." Luigi flushed and said nothing.

At first they danced with a decent interval between their bodies, but gradually, as if by mutual and unspoken agreement, they came closer together, until finally their cheeks too touched. They said nothing, but he could feel her body responding to his in a way that reminded him of Stephanie in the early days of their courtship, when she had been able to rouse him by the slightest pressure of her body against his, or an almost imperceptible shift of position. Occasionally he glanced uneasily over at Dorothy, but she seemed to be paying no attention to them and was deep in conversation with Luigi. When the music ended, they stood together side by side, still holding hands; he felt her squeeze his palm tightly, then relax her grip. The lights came up again and the band launched into an ancient rock and roll number; they danced apart this time, not looking at each other.

The band took its break and they returned to the table, where Roger asked Eva to order more wine. At the table next to them a party of eight had been eating and drinking lavishly, to the accompaniment of a good deal of noise and laughter. Suddenly the good humour changed to antagonism and the sound of quarrelling; the man sitting closest to Roger grabbed his neighbour by the collar and dragged him from his seat onto the floor, almost knocking Roger's chair over as he did so. He stood up and began to haul the other man across the floor on his back, towards the door; neither of them spoke, the victim offered no resistance and, after a moment's silence, their companions returned to their talk and laughter, nor did nay any of the waiters attempt to intervene. They disappeared through the door and, in an instant, the assailant returned, wiping his palms together, and calmly resumed his place at the table.

"Good God!" Roger exclaimed. "What was going on there?"

"Peasants," Eva replied scornfully. "They come in from the villages just to get drunk. They are nothing but pigs; they have no manners."

"*My* family were peasants," Luigi muttered, almost inaudibly, but Eva ignored him. The wine arrived and Roger offered it round. Both Dorothy and Luigi shook their heads; he shrugged and refilled his and Eva's glasses. The band started to play once more and he invited Dorothy to dance. She shook her head, saying it was too crowded and wasn't any fun. He hesitated and then asked Eva, who accepted immediately. They stayed together for all four numbers, standing side by side in the intervals, hidden among the other dancers, with hands clasped.

When they returned to the table, Dorothy said that she wanted to leave: She was tired and had a headache; there was too much noise, heat and cigarette smoke. Though both Eva and Luigi, he noticed, had refrained from smoking, the air in the room was thick and hazy with smoke and even he felt uncomfortable with it. He got ready to accompany her, but she told him to stay and enjoy himself: Luigi would go with her, he wasn't having much fun either. He protested feebly, then acquiesced, promising that he wouldn't be long.

As soon as they left, Eva lit a cigarette and offered him one. "I couldn't stand that much longer," she sighed, blissfully emitting a long stream of smoke. Though he was not quite certain what she was referring to, he nodded in agreement.

"Are you asleep?" he whispered, as he entered the bedroom an hour later.

"It's all right. You can put the light on."

"I'm sorry you didn't enjoy it." He sat down on the edge of the bed and began to remove his shoes. "I always thought you liked dancing, though I agree the band was pretty terrible."

"It wasn't just the band, as you well know. But I don't want to talk about it now."

He felt aggrieved, for nothing much had happened after she left. What else did she expect when she refused to dance with him and Luigi had been such a wet blanket, ignoring Eva? Unless that had been a device so that she and Luigi could go off together. He remembered escorting Eva home and assuring her rather drunkenly that, though he liked her very much, he still loved his wife and, even though they had problems, they were going to work them out. And then there had been a friendly good-night kiss and that was that.

He got into bed and tried to embrace her as usual, but she turned away, with her back to him. He lay still for a moment, staring up at the ceiling. "You won't believe this," he said, "but remember what happened at that table next to us, the fellow who dragged the other man out of the room?" He paused and, when she said nothing, continued: "Well, exactly the same thing happened all over again. The second man came back, just after you left, and sat down again as if nothing had happened. And then, half an hour later, without any warning, his friend grabbed him again, yanked him out of his seat and pulled him out of the room, and once again no one took any notice or tried to stop him."

He waited for a response and, when she made none, said good night.

"Good night," she muttered.

He found it hard for once to get to sleep, thinking over the events of the evening, and then, just as he was about to go off, he heard a fly buzzing frantically over at the window and hurling itself repeatedly at the glass. He tried to ignore it, but it only became more and more agitated, zooming around the room, skimming his head and charging despairingly at the glass once more.

"For Christ's sake," he groaned finally, hauling himself out of bed and looking for something with which to swat it. "The window's wide open, why can't it find its way out?" Moonlight gleamed on the lake, and the insect was a tiny black blob on the windowpane.

"Don't hurt it," Dorothy murmured sleepily as he was about to strike, "it's trying to tell you something."

✠✠✠MARGARET✠✠✠

My *Christ in Glory* was unveiled two days ago, to predictable
enough acclaim, the Duke and the Bishop both being present
to savour the flattering—yet not quite sycophantic—depiction
of them kneeling with due humility at the foot of his throne,
yet looking sturdily conscious of their own worth and dignity
even in this exalted company. I accepted the praise and congratulations with due modesty, fully aware of the trivial, even
mechanical quality of the piece itself—nothing to be ashamed
of, a competent, craftsmanlike effort, yet totally routine in
every respect and without an ounce of true commitment or
feeling to be found in it. I knew well enough, however, that
this was exactly what was needed at this stage: something that
displayed my technical skill and impeccably orthodox mental-
ity, with nothing disconcertingly eccentric or controversial to
make them wonder what they might be letting themselves in
for in future.

The Bishop was very gracious with me in his clumsy, elephantine way, allowing me to kiss his hand—or what little of
it was not covered with rings and precious stones—and only
just stopping himself from patting me on the head as he murmured his congratulations. "You have performed a marvellous
and invaluable service, dear lady," he told me, "and generations yet to come will bless you for the uplifting vision you
have offered them."

The Duke, to his credit, was not taken in quite so easily, as
he made clear that evening in the privacy of his bedchamber.
"Certainly you have avoided offending them," he remarked,
"but, to anyone with the slightest aesthetic sensibility—fortunately a rare commodity in these parts—you seem almost to be
laughing at them by presenting so precisely and pedantically

exactly what they want. I appreciate your reasons for this, but too much of this stuff will begin to look uncomfortably like satire, and then where will you be?"

I assured him that I was aware of this risk and that my strategy was to begin to incorporate some technical experiments into otherwise orthodox subject matter, feeling my way gradually towards a greater freedom that would eventually infiltrate *what* I was painting as well as *how* I was painting it. In the meantime, my *real* work would be confined to my sketchbook and, once I felt confident—or desperate—enough, I would start to work up the material there, first into the background of larger paintings and finally into their very substance.

That method too had its dangers, he observed after a pause, not so much of discovery of my real intentions as that the habit of subterfuge—or, not to put too fine a point upon it, intellectual dishonesty—might infect my "real" work and distort it, perhaps fatally. It might be far from easy to keep the two strands distinct and separate: What I saw now as a necessary compromise might become, without my noticing it, my normal state of mind.

I had no alternative, I told him stiffly. Would he prefer me to be silent altogether? Realising I was close to tears, he apologised for haranguing me and began to soothe and comfort me instead, so that the evening ended, to our mutual satisfaction, in the accustomed way.

As the Duke's visit coincided with a feast day devoted to the memory of some obscure saint martyred in a peculiarly ingenious and unpleasant manner, there were endless processions through the streets the next morning in which the various town dignitaries, both secular and ecclesiastical, paraded in masks and elaborate costumes, generally representing figures from biblical history or local legend. As a mark of especial favour, those of us who had behaved with conspicuous sycophancy towards the Abbess in recent weeks were permitted to witness these and even mingle with the crowds; to my amazement, I was included among those so honoured, no doubt in grudging acknowledgement of the Duke's presence and the official approbation of my painting.

The various disguises worn by the participants intrigued me: In many cases it was as if they were living out fantasies suppressed in their everyday existence and now allowed briefly, and with impunity, to run riot. Although only men were officially permitted to take part, many of the floats seemed at first sight to be packed with women, fantastically coiffed and costumed, painted, powdered and bejewelled, posturing, simpering and blowing effusive kisses to the crowd. Even when they passed close by me, it was almost impossible to be certain that they must indeed all be men: The illusion was perfect, the disguise so intricately and patiently conceived. Rejoicing in their anonymity, many of them fondled and caressed each other, often with embarrassingly explicit and even obscene gestures—actions that, if performed at any other time, would have ensured at best a whipping and at worst a hanging. They could not *all*, I mused, be genuine sodomites, though I was not so naive as to ignore the existence of a substantial number of these beneath the placid surface of respectable town society; many husbands, many merchants, soldiers, servants, craftsmen, apprentices, peasants, even priests, must find release of something hidden or suppressed inside them for a few brief days like this each year.

Few of these exhibits made any pretence of representing a theme or story, biblical or otherwise, and those that did often performed a surprising reversal of the expected roles. Notorious prostitutes—or so I gathered from the scandalised comments of the women and the appreciative acknowledgements of the men around me—paraded themselves as saints or Old Testament heroines such as Ruth or Sarah. Judith and Susanna, as near naked as the remaining shreds of decency allowed, made numerous appearances, as did various classical scenes in which scantily dressed maidens barely evaded or willingly submitted to the advances of heftily muscled—and equally skimpily clad—males and an astonishingly varied assortment of animals and birds.

Even ecclesiastical dignitaries seemed to enter freely into the spirit of riot and disorder, the most astonishing sight being the Bishop himself, dressed as Bacchus and wearing a crown of vine leaves, lolling half-naked on a couch with his immense paunch spilling everywhere, imbibing huge draughts from a flagon of wine that he would then wave cheerfully above his head before swilling once more, while he smeared grapes and sweetmeats into his mouth with his other hand. His fat fingers were still covered with rings that flashed and sparkled in the sunlight with every move he made, especially when he would suspend his eating and drinking to caress the group of acolytes who surrounded him, boys no more than ten years old, dressed only in loincloths, whose shrill voices accompanied the music of lutes and viols in what I recognised to be obscene Latin lyrics. Everyone knew him, everyone applauded, and yet the next morning he performed solemn mass as usual and delivered a thunderous sermon condemning all manner of fornication and sodomy, hurling threats of eternal damnation at any who succumbed.

In the afternoon the festivities continued with the setting up of fairground booths and theatrical performances in the field on the edge of town where the executions are normally held. Brightly dressed Gypsies—tolerated on this occasion though usually held in the utmost suspicion and regularly driven out of town—told fortunes, promising their gullible listeners wealth, success and eternal happiness in love. Men competed in contests of archery, horsemanship and jousting, attempting, often with considerable success, to break each other's heads open with massive staves. Wives accused of nagging or other shrewish behaviour were ducked in a nearby pond to the accompaniment of much mirth and jesting from bystanders, until they emerged spluttering and half-drowned, gasping out promises never to offend again. Itinerant minstrels and ballad singers performed their latest compositions and attempted to hawk copies of their poems and songs. A bear danced ponderously to the music of a flute while men laid eager wagers on the outcome of a cockfight nearby. Self-proclaimed artists drew portraits of children and babies to whom they attributed angelic features that should have rendered them unrecognisable to their parents, yet the drawings were immediately purchased on the spot for exorbitant sums of money. Alternatively, they would produce flattering pictures of young women with whom they then attempted to arrange assignations for later in the evening. I was tempted to offer to try my hand at this for, trite as the results are, this kind of work demands a certain degree of practical skill, but my nun's clothing created an insuperable barrier even to the idea, just as it inhibited me from asking one of the Gypsies to tell my fortune and promise me a dark and handsome husband and a dozen sturdy children.

There were also puppet shows, usually crudely costumed and performed, repeating with minimal variation themes of marital strife and conflict—to the uproarious delight of at least the males in the audience. But one of these shows was different—elaborately designed and costumed and operated with considerable skill; it also told a less predictable story, one that, as a chill of recognition spread slowly through my body, I began to associate with myself. A father orders his daughter to marry a rich merchant; she refuses and runs away with her lover; her father and brothers pursue them and kill the lover; the daughter is sent to a convent. Here she contrives to attract the attention of a king (doubtless, I suspected, a prudent substitute for the Duke) and literally spreads her legs for him—a scene portrayed in graphic detail and the first lapse of taste in what had been till then a remarkably restrained production. She is rewarded with gifts of jewellery and fine clothing, she grows proud and arrogant, she vents her spite on the kindly and sweet-natured Abbess, going so far as to secretly kill her pet dog and have it served up to her in a pie—and then gleefully reveals what she has done. Increasingly, I become a monster, permitted to indulge my every whim of cruelty and revenge. Bodies pile up around me as I cackle hideously in maniacal frenzy—until finally God lends a hand in the form of a well-aimed thunderbolt and the deluded king returns to his senses, receives absolution and reigns happily ever afterwards.

There was no mention of painting—the villainess had no redeeming qualities and cared only for material and sensual gratification—but surely it was intended to be my story? I gazed around me cautiously, but no one in the appreciative audience seemed to associate me with the character and, if my eyes met theirs, they flicked indifferently past with no more than the usual sign of disapproval or hostility. Perhaps I was identifying too closely: The performers, after all, were strangers to the district and could scarcely have known my history in advance, and many of the incidents were traditional and even commonplace enough—there must be innumerable disobedient daughters unwillingly confined to convents, and the good but naive ruler led astray by sensual passion and ensnared by an evil and self-seeking mistress is a familiar, even threadbare trope. The only worrying detail was the Abbess and her dog, but even that probably had its analogies elsewhere. I breathed more easily: I am hardly unique, after all; my story, in at least its outlines, must be repeated, with subtle variations, in many other places, at many other times.

As evening drew on, the theatrical performances took over, lit by sputtering oil lamps and flickering candles that sent shadows darting and sweeping over the perfomers. Most, like the puppet shows, were gross and predictable yet, in their own way, undeniably amusing: dull, boorish, authoritarian old husbands, deservedly cuckolded by their sexually rampant young wives and the latters' handsome and ingenious lovers. A good deal of concealment behind doors and in closets, bathtubs, barrels and cellars; hair's-breadth escapes from discovery; disguises, wigs and false noses; hearty beatings administered to fools and lechers as bystanders snigger and applaud; repentance and reformation—or sometimes the flouting of all moral law as the tricksters and adulterers triumph and blatantly continue their activities before the very eyes of their defeated and demoralised opponents. Harlequin's guile and inventiveness, his grace and clumsiness, his childlike extremes of misery and ecstasy. And then, slicing through the coarseness, the guffaws, the vulgar exhibitionism, the double meanings—the melancholy poetry of Pierrot, his sad attachment to Columbine, his hopeless love, his impossible idealism, his tears, his never-to-be-fulfilled dreams.

As if subdued and moved by this, the audience begins to drift away as darkness deepens, pairing off into couples but without the raucous laughter, the horseplay, the flagrant challenges, the exaggerated giggles, the lewd invitations and simulated modesty that prevailed earlier in the day. What little conversation can be heard is quiet and thoughtful and, as the couples drop to the ground at the edge of the field, the air seems to quiver with the intensity and purity of their passion. I stand listening till I can bear it no longer and run blindly back to town and the illusory security of my cell.

And then, the next morning, it was back to business as usual: Before leaving, the Duke and the Bishop presided over the execution of a group of heretics whose sceptical opinions on the real presence of the body of Christ in the Eucharist have caused considerable scandal over the past few months—in the eyes of the church at least and, through her, to a largely uncomprehending but dutifully submissive public. This time attendance was a duty, not a privilege, and though I feel personally that these people's views have much to recommend them and are indeed harmless enough, I had the good sense to keep my opinions to myself—a wise precaution given the vicious hatred directed at them by the local rabble as they were led towards their deaths.

They were lined up neatly on the top of a huge pyre, all six of them, three men and three women, side by side, and were denied a last request to embrace each other before being bound to the stake. The wood was damp and took some time to catch properly, and they were soon hidden from view by clouds of billowing smoke—to the vociferous disgust of the crowd around me, deprived of the exemplary spectacle of the victims' agonised writhings. They must have died of asphyxiation long before the flames actually reached them: I heard them praying loudly and fervently for some time and calling out words of comfort to one another, until the smoke enveloped them and their voices gave way to smothered choking and coughing. Long before the end, my companions started to leave, muttering discontentedly at the failure of the authorities to conduct these increasingly frequent occasions with proper zeal and efficiency.

The leader of the group, a nobleman, had been spared the stake by privilege of his rank and was quickly despatched by the headsman at the beginning of the ceremony, in full view of the associates he was assumed to have led astray. As I have been planning for some time a painting on the topic of Judith and Holofernes—or at least a series of sketches that one day *will* be a painting—I had made prior arrangements through the Duke for the head to be delivered, privately and confidentially, to my cell so that I could begin work and I spent most of the remainder of the day studying and drawing it.

I was curious to know Dimitrios's response to the success of my "Christ," especially as we had engaged in long and bitter argument over the correct method of preparing the walls before the paint was applied and the work even begun. He had agreed, after much grumbling, to undertake the laborious task of smoothing the rough stone with sand and properly aged lime, insisting as he did so that I was being unnecessarily scrupulous and fussy in my demands; but when it came to applying the plaster, he turned openly surly and uncooperative. I was determined to follow the advice of the master craftsman: "Hurl the first, and coarsest, coat of plaster onto the surface roughly and vigorously from the trowel and then spread it with short, pounding blows in a rapid series of brusque, nervous strokes." Not so, claimed Dimitrios. His father had been a master mason (an unlikely story that I have failed so far to confirm) and he had *always* applied the plaster in a careful succession of smooth, elegant, graceful movements. Later on, by the third and final coat, I told him, such finessse would be appropriate; applied throughout, however, it would fail to produce the porous effect that was essential if the wall were to hold and assimilate the paint. I was forced to prove my point by allowing him to do it his way, while I prepared another section of wall properly, and then conducting tests on both areas; we wasted almost a week on this, but he was finally convinced by the results and we worked in harmony from then on.

He had offered little comment on the painting when it was finished, apart from conceding that it was "all right"; instead, he asked me suddenly if I believed in reincarnation. If he meant Resurrection, I replied, or eternal life, of the kind depicted in the picture, I suppose I did. Didn't everyone?

No, he said impatiently, he was talking about something entirely different: the idea that after each life we were reborn in a different body and lived through another existence.

I had encountered speculation of this kind, I replied warily (the arrest and execution of the heretics having made me cautious of articulating unorthodox ideas), mainly through my study of Plato while I lived at home. It was an interesting, but surely unsubstantiated, concept.

He had met philosophers, he continued, in the Orient, who believed in it implicitly, believed that we all live thousands of lives, each of them merely a dream of the "real" life, which we leave in order to come into this one and to which we return when we die. After each life, depending on our moral behaviour in each existence, we are reborn in a higher or lower form—perhaps even that of an animal, bird or insect. The aim, of course, is to reach a higher stage each time until, after centuries or even millennia have passed, we finally attain the state of enlightenment that allows us to retire, so to speak, from the whole process.

And what happens, I enquired, once everyone has been enlightened?

Then, presumably, the purpose of the universe has been attained and time will come to an end; we will live forever in infinity. His own version, however, was rather different, for it was his belief that the universe itself was eternal and would *never* come to an end. There would be no Day of Judgement, followed by an eternity of heaven or hell; rather, every creature would be endlessly reborn, in a different form, until each of us had assumed every possible identity that the world had to offer. But, as new life was constantly being created, this was a process that could never be finished and would continue, literally, throughout eternity.

I thought this over for a moment: Do you mean, I suggested, that rather than moving on sequentially from one life to the next, each of us will have a turn at being everyone who has ever existed, or ever will exist? I will be you and the Duke and the Abbess and the Bishop and each of my brothers and my father and my mother and Stefan and millions of other people both in the past and in the future, and you will likewise be me and all these other people too?

Something like that, he agreed, except that it's not just limited to people. Each of us will be every animal and bird and fish and insect that has ever existed, every tree and flower and bush, every leaf and twig of every tree, every rock, every stone, every stream, every pond, every drop of rain that falls into these streams and ponds, every grain of sand on the beach and every wave breaking over the sand, every star, every cloud and every rainbow.

I gazed at him in amazement, wondering if he had gone mad. That would take forever, I protested.

Exactly. He smiled happily. That's just my point.

Then I remembered something. How does that fit, I asked, with what you were saying about flies surviving us after the Day of Judgement, if you don't believe the world will come to an end?

I'll tell you later, he said. It's all very complicated and I'm not sure I've worked it out properly yet. Give me a week or two longer.

By that time you might be standing on the pyre beside the other heretics, I reminded him. You can trust *me*, but, for heaven's sake, don't breathe a word of this to anyone else.

Although he had, of course, seen my *Christ in Glory* when it was completed, he was far too lowly a figure to be invited to the unveiling and he received my somewhat smug recital of the praise that had been heaped upon it with visible impatience. "It's good," he acknowledged finally, "but hardly worthy of your talent. I've seen some of your sketches and there's ten times more vitality and passion in them than there is here."

I pretended to take offence at this, for I had no intention of encouraging him to get above himself and start to pass judgement on my work, yet his words matched so closely my own inner feelings and the opinions of the Duke that my indignation must have carried little conviction.

"What's this?" he went on brashly, taking advantage of my indecision and beginning to unwrap the head that I had brought into the church with me, intending to continue sketching it while he prepared the wall for my next official painting, a Nativity. I told him sharply to leave it alone, but it was too late.

"So it's true what they say after all," he remarked, with a low whistle of surprise. "You *do* get the Duke to order executions for your benefit."

"That's nonsense," I said, pulling the cloth back over the distorted features. "The man was going to die anyway; it was nothing to do with me." I was aware of these rumours, for people had noticed me sketching some of the victims at the various executions that punctuate our life here with such agreeable regularity and a few had made disparaging comments, calling me a "ghoul" and a "vampire." To avoid hostility I had begun to operate more discreetly but, short of getting whole bodies delivered to my cell, there was no way of evading attention completely.

His words also reminded me of the puppet show, whose central figure had revelled in having people put to death in various graphically disagreeable ways.

"It's for my *Last Judgement*," I lied defensively, "like all my other sketches. How do you suppose I can terrify sinners into repentance if I don't make the torments of hell as vivid and gruesome as possible?"

"That's not your real reason, is it? That's just for public consumption. You're not really interested in frightening people or saving their souls. There's something else behind it."

"Aesthetics," I said. "I want my work to be as truthful and realistic as possible. If that involves confronting pain and ugliness, so be it."

"You do mean 'confronting,' don't you, rather than 'enjoying'?"

I bridled at this: "Why should I enjoy seeing people suffer?"

"Maybe 'enjoy' is the wrong word. You certainly seem fascinated by it."

"I record the world as it is. It's not a pleasant sight, you know. I could paint far worse things if I wanted. Anyway, I've had enough of talking about this; why don't you get on with your work?"

He began to obey reluctantly. "I could help you, you know," he suggested. "I have friends in high places." I ignored him, turning my back obtrusively and, after a moment, he set to work.

He had upset me nevertheless and I found it difficult to concentrate on my drawing. The man had gone to his death serenely enough, but there was nothing peaceful in those staring eyes and that gaping mouth. Should I ignore this and paint the "inner" truth of a soul reconciled to its fate and expiring confident of its own righteousness and eventual salvation? No doubt this was what Sister Maria would recommend. But I was using him to depict Holofernes, a monster and a tyrant who fully deserved his fate, so inner and outer truth were in perfect harmony. Except that I was using as my model not the real Holofernes, but a kind and decent man. . . .

I abandoned this useless speculation and returned to Dimitrios's central allegation: that I took a cruel and morbid delight in watching and recording the suffering of others. Watching, no: I had to force myself to keep my eyes open and rarely succeeded even in doing that. But recording, once it was all over, perhaps. The pain and the death were not my fault and there was certainly a genuine pleasure in capturing every trace and nuance that they had left behind. But did the pleasure extend beyond that, as Dimitrios had charged? And even if it did, was that not justified if I aroused a genuine revulsion in others, a desire to put an end to the constant and unnecessary cruelty that surrounds us every day? A desire that I know I share myself.

Once again I gave up and tried to think of something else, the Nativity that I had promised as my next work. I had intended to use my sketches of Sister Helena as the basis for the Virgin, but now I began to question the wisdom of this. Despite Sister Maria's approval, I could easily be accused of mocking and insulting the holy image; it might be wiser to play safe once more and provide something more familiar, especially if unpleasant gossip was circulating about me already. Later on, when I was more established, things would be different. Yes, I know, I mentally addressed an invisible Duke, I can compromise once too often; but wasn't it also you who warned me not to shock them too obviously or too soon?

I sighed, dragged out the half-finished sketches I had made of Angelica and began reluctantly to elaborate them. After a time Dimitrios abandoned his halfhearted pretence of working on the wall surface and came to peer over my shoulder. Normally I detest being watched as I am working, but I felt that he was silently offering a truce and had no wish to offend him unnecessarily. "Don't come too close," I warned him, as a compromise, "or Brother Milo will get ideas."

Brother Milo, at the Abbess's insistence, acted as our chaperone whenever we were alone together. He was supremely unfitted—or, from another point of view, ideal—for that function, being totally deaf and half-blind; he spent all his time sitting mumbling prayers and fingering his rosary, and it would have taken little short of an earthquake to attract his attention elsewhere. He usually had to be roused by one of us at the end of the day, when Dimitrios led him gently back to his cell. No doubt the Abbess chose him for reasons of propriety: to leave me alone with *two* able-bodied men would surely, in her eyes, have been an open invitation to an endless and unbridled orgy and, though she would certainly have welcomed my personal disgrace, the reputation of the abbey was also at stake and had to be considered.

Dimitrios ignored my comment. "It's quite good," he ventured after a moment, "but isn't it rather too sickly—Raphael gone to seed?"

I was tempted to tell him to mind his own business, but once again he had nudged against my own misgivings. "Give me time," I said. "A few more months of this stuff and then they'll stop watching me so closely and I'll be free to do what I want."

He shook his head. "By then it will be too late," he told me bluntly, echoing the Duke.

"All right." I was irritated by his air of certainty. "No one ever looks at the background of a painting like this. Suppose I put in some scenes of daily life—people harvesting, children playing, a boy climbing a tree to steal apples, women doing laundry on the riverbank. And among them will be a crowd standing round a bonfire, and in the middle of the bonfire will be people tied to stakes and burning to death."

"Too direct." He shook his head once more. "I get your point—the two faces of the church, it's obvious enough—but I wouldn't give much for your chances if anyone ever explained it to the Bishop."

"It doesn't *have* to be taken as a criticism. I could always say it represented the eternal vigilance of the church in defending its ideals. Heresy must always be rooted out. And the Virgin represents God's mercy even when his servants are inflicting exemplary punishment on offenders for their own good."

"That *might* work, provided you have a good lawyer on your side. If you're ambiguous enough, you can get away with anything."

"If you're still worried, I can make it even more ambiguous. I won't show exactly *what* it is they're burning—just a few dots that might or might not be people. But I'll put a priest and some soldiers in the forefront of the crowd and anyone looking at it can draw their own conclusions. Especially after what's been going on here recently."

"Don't get *too* ambiguous, though. What's the use if you're so subtle that no one gets the point at all?"

FOUR

As soon as she got back to the church, she went over to study the painting again. Yes, there in the background, so tiny that she had hardly noticed it before, was a crowd standing round something that was certainly a bonfire, though it was quite impossible to tell what was burning inside it. With some effort, and guided by her reading of the journals, she could make out what might well be a priest and a soldier or two, though, without that assistance, they would have been virtually unidentifiable. The painting was dominated by the angelic features of the Virgin, sweet and serene, to be sure, but "nudged" as Margaret had put it, by Dimitrios's reservations, it now seemed *too* pretty, *too* self-consciously idealised.

She wondered, for the first time, whether Dimitrios had ever really existed, or whether Margaret had invented him as a means of articulating to herself, and arguing out, her own inner debates about her work—and also indulging in some farfetched and potentially dangerous intellectual speculations.

101

Perhaps she had compromised once again on this work, covering her tracks so thoroughly that—as Dimitrios/Margaret had warned her—she had ended up obscuring the meaning so totally that only someone already initiated would understand it. Dorothy let her gaze wander over the other background details: The men were harvesting, the women doing their laundry, the children playing. Yet there was another incident she had previously overlooked—a woman, tiny in scale but with features clearly contorted with rage, mercilessly beating a small boy with a stick, possibly for stealing fruit, for he clutched something in his hand and half a dozen apples or pears were scattered at his feet. There, no doubt, was Margaret's solution to her dilemma: If her nerve failed her at the last moment in one respect, this was compensated by a contrast of another kind—the public and private faces of motherhood. And, with this detail in mind, the syrupy sweetness of the Virgin became deliberately overdone— even, from a certain perspective, masking a hidden evil.

This conclusion disturbed her nevertheless and she had to ask herself why. It was one thing to attack the church for its hypocrisy, another to show mothers beating their own children. Roger would have had an answer for this: Current orthodoxy allowed open season on the church, with very little risk of retribution, while it was heresy to suggest that women were ever aggressors rather than victims. He could point from his own experience—and he had said this often enough—to numerous examples of child abuse and violence against husbands carried out by women, yet these were either ignored in polemics on the subject or so surrounded by excuses and rationalisations that they somehow became almost admirable, acts of justifiable defiance against, as he put it, the stereotyped bogeyman of patriarchy.

Without agreeing with him totally, she felt uneasily that he had a point and this contributed to her own disquiet with the picture. She could understand why Margaret had toned down the burning of the heretics to almost complete obscurity, for the risks she was taking were enormous; yet she found it difficult to accept the substitution of a kind of treachery against her own sex from someone she had come to see as being on her own side and sharing many of her values.

Her musings were interrupted by Luigi, who announced that they enjoyed the rare privilege of being invited to lunch by his boss. "It's an opportunity not be missed," he informed her. "He is a renowned gourmet and employs the finest chef in the region; he also has a fabulous wine cellar—one that somehow survived the siege. I would forget about doing any work this afternoon, if I were you."

She accepted at once but asked if Roger and Eva would be coming too: They had arranged to meet them for lunch, as usual. Luigi replied evasively that they hadn't been invited, yet his tone implied that, if he had wanted to include them, this could have been arranged. "They'll get on well enough without us," he added, with a touch of bitterness. Though he had said nothing explicit as they walked back to the hotel the previous evening, his behaviour during the dance had clearly revealed to her his unhappy awareness of the other couple's mutual attraction.

"What does Roger do all day?" he asked, as if sounding out her own feelings on the subject, and with the unspoken quali-fication "when he's not with Eva." She replied that he wandered around, looking at things "though he always somehow seems to end up at the torture museum."

When Luigi expressed surprise, she said there was probably a reason for this. "His father was a prisoner of war of the Japan-ese and died in a forced labour camp in Thailand—beaten to death for failing to perform some impossible task when he was already half-dead with dysentery. Roger never really knew him, he was too young, and he never took much interest in what happened to him until recently, when he suddenly began to read books on the subject. I wouldn't say he's become obsessed with it, but he seems to be trying to come to terms with something that's been unconsciously bottled up inside him for a long time.

"Actually," she continued thoughtfully, "something in Margaret's journals reminded me of a passage in one of the books he showed me. In some of the better camps the prisoners were allowed to perform theatricals and they were extraordinarily ingenious in making costumes and sets from the scraps of material they had available. The biggest hit was always the men who managed to dress themselves up convincingly as women, with wigs, makeup, clothes and everything. It reminded me of that beautiful moment in *La Grande Illusion* when the prisoners in a German camp do the same thing and this 'woman' makes her entrance and suddenly everyone goes very quiet and solemn, almost awestruck."

"It's a wonderful film," he said. "We used to have a film club here where I saw that and lots of other classics. I don't know if it will ever start up again now."

He became more lighthearted as they approached the museum. "Be prepared for some of our local specialities," he warned her. "Newborn puppies gently seethed in their mother's milk; eels from the lake skinned alive, tossed in boiling oil for a few seconds and delivered still wriggling to your plate. I'm only teasing," he added, amused at her horrified reaction, "but he's almost certain to come up with something unusual, even if it's not on that scale."

To her surprise, their host was fully dressed and was already seated at table. He made a gesture of rising to welcome them, but slumped quickly back into his chair before it was completed. He waved Dorothy into a seat at his right hand; his fingers, she noticed, were forested with magnificent jewels, clustered together so thickly that the flesh was almost invisible. She was reminded of Margaret's description of the Bishop and wondered if this man was somehow a descendant—vows of chastity counted for little among the privileged clergy of the time. The table was set for five and, after a pause, the curator asked whether their friends would be delayed much longer; with an embarrassed smile, and avoiding her eyes, Luigi said they sent their apologies but had an unfortunate previous engagement.

The food, as predicted, was magnificent and the wine even better. Dorothy was accustomed to good wine, as Roger fancied himself a connoisseur, but this surpassed anything she had ever tasted. When she asked where it came from, she was told that it was local and over fifty years old. "It doesn't travel well," the curator explained, "and is never exported." She ate warily, attempting to identify each dish; most were recognisable but it was only after she had finished the most delicious of them that the curator announced delightedly that she had just eaten hedgehog—"a traditional Gypsy recipe that only my chef knows how to prepare properly." He went on to discuss the "problem" of the Gypsies, despised and displaced by both sides in the recent conflict. They had "flooded" into the town and it was proving "impossible" to get rid of them. They were dirty, smelly and uncivilised, even (he apologised for putting it so bluntly at table) urinating and defecating openly in the streets; they lived by theft and begging and were responsible for most of the local crime and prostitution, even selling their own small children. It was time someone took the matter in hand and got rid of them; if the authorities failed to act soon, public-minded citizens would have to take the initiative on their own and teach them a good lesson.

Luigi kept his eyes lowered during this diatribe and seemed as embarrassed by it as she was. She was reminded of endless dinner parties with people important to Roger's career, where she was expected to listen in silence to similar outbursts of prejudice, because to object would jeopardise a valuable connection or contact. Roger was always apologetic afterwards, saying that he was as disgusted as she was, but he had to deal with people of all kinds and couldn't always afford to make fine distinctions. And here she experienced the same helplessness, unwilling to offend someone whose guest she was and who was treating her—by his own lights—with exemplary kindness.

After the meal they retired to the study in which she had first been introduced to their host, where he reclined gracefully on his sofa and, with a flash of his ringed hand, invited them to help themselves to a bewildering array of liqueurs on the table at his side. With a perfunctory request for "the dear lady's" permission—which she felt unable to refuse—he lit a cigar for himself and offered one to Luigi. Giving a quick glance at Dorothy, he declined; she had finally, after much hesitation, screwed up the courage to ask him not to smoke while they were working together and had been embarrassed by the extent of his contrition and the repeated apologies for his insensitivity in not having thought of her discomfort earlier.

Having ignored the subject throughout the meal, the curator now asked her languidly about her work on the frescoes. Luigi, after offering to help her examine the undamaged wall for signs of a painting concealed behind it, seemed—whether intentionally or not—to have forgotten all about the subject, and the promised hammer and chisel had never materialised. Partly to jog his memory, she asked her host whether he believed the various legends that had clustered around Margaret's life and whether it was possible that her paintings of paradise and hell might still exist.

"Mere rumours, dear lady, concocted for the amusement of gullible tourists," he assured her loftily, with a wave of his cigar that sent smoke swirling dangerously close to her face. "Like everything else associated with that mythical personage."

"Why do you say 'mythical'?"

"Because there is no evidence whatsoever that she actually painted anything." Forestalling her objections, he acknowledged, with another waft of smoke that set her coughing, that the woman had doubtless existed, as a nun and as the Duke's mistress, but not as a painter. Though he had not yet enjoyed the opportunity to examine the works in person, if the reports as to their quality were correct, they could have been painted only by a man.

"What about her journals? She talks in detail about how each work was created."

He shrugged. "A combination of jealousy and hysteria. She was a woman capable of, let us say, extreme and irrational emotional turmoil, even instability. She was renowned for her promiscuity and may well have fallen in love with the *real* painter, either a local monk or some transient visitor, and, being rejected by him, compensated by claiming his work as her own."

"Why does the obvious explanation—that she really painted them—have to be rejected in favour of some quasi-sexual rationalisation? You just need to *look* at the work," she continued, struggling to avoid open rudeness, "to see that only a woman could have created it."

He shrugged once more. "As you wish, dear lady," he conceded politely, but with obvious insincerity. "I submit, as always, to the spell of female charm. You are, after all, the expert, and I am merely a humble bureaucrat." Changing the subject, he offered another liqueur, which she refused, and they left shortly afterwards.

Once they were in the street, she released her pent-up anger on Luigi. "They always win, don't they? First they say there aren't any paintings and this hysterical female imagined creating them. When they have to acknowledge the paintings exist, they say someone else did them, and this hysterical, jealous, promiscuous, crazy female for some obscure reason tried to claim them as her own. And when you try to point out the facts, they retreat into offering sleazy, oozing 'compliments' on 'female charm' that are little short of insulting and are supposed to make you feel so good—or so insignificant—that you stop trying to think for yourself any longer."

"I'm sorry. It was a mistake to take you there. But I felt I could hardly refuse the invitation."

"It's all right, it's not your fault. And, in a way, it was quite instructive. It reminds me of what I'm going to be up against trying to get her work accepted back home—condescending put-downs by the male old guard on the one hand, and attempts to turn her into a forerunner of hard-line feminism by the other side. That's the way I'd been beginning to think of her myself, in fact, but now I'm starting to wonder."

"What do you mean?"

"Come, and I'll show you."

"Where the hell have they got to? They're half an hour late already." He looked at his watch for the tenth time in the past five minutes.

"They're probably engrossed in something to do with their beloved Margaret and have forgotten all about the time. Does it really matter anyway?" Eva smiled at him flirtatiously.

"Probably not, it's just pretty rude. I suppose we'd better order then. Do you want another drink?"

"Some wine, perhaps. But why don't we go somewhere else to eat? This place is so boring. There's a nice restaurant on the other side of the lake if you can wait another half hour before eating."

"Why not? I've waited long enough already."

He drove somewhat unsteadily, the ubiquitous brandy, served before, after and—for the locals—during meals, having gone somewhat to his head. After initial dislike, he was beginning to acquire a taste for it and was drinking it rather more frequently than he knew he should. Eva had offered to drive, but he had waved her aside, saying he felt all right, and she had accepted his decision demurely. Fortunately, there was virtually no other traffic on the road and, after a few minutes, he began to relax. Sunlight sparkled peacefully on the lake to their right and the mountains loomed on the other side, seemingly calm yet containing a potential for violence and terror that could be unleashed again at any moment.

"Tell me about the caves," he said suddenly. "That journalist mentioned them."

"What about them?"

"He said the terrorists were still hiding there."

"There's not much to say about them. People fleeing persecution have used them for centuries. Hermits and outcasts lived in them. Criminals were exiled there. And now, maybe, the terrorists are hiding there. Who knows?"

"Do *you*?" He had meant to be more cunning than this, but the alcohol had blurred his thinking.

"How should I?"

He tried to extricate himself, but only got in deeper. "Adam thought you might have contacts there."

She turned away and when she looked back at him a tear glinted in her eye. She brushed it away with her hand. "I suppose I should have told you earlier; I have a lover there. It's like Romeo and Juliet. His family and mine have been feuding for decades, perhaps centuries. We could never marry and live together the way things are just now. It probably sounds horribly primitive to you, but it's part of how we have to live here.

"I know what you're thinking, about Luigi," she went on, with something like a sob in her voice, "and you've probably heard other rumours about me. But I've told you already that Luigi is nothing more to me than a friend. I'm not such a bad person really."

He felt embarrassed at her obvious attempt to manipulate him and the amateurish melodrama of her performance; yet this awareness served only to increase the desire he felt for her. If she wanted to play games, that was all right by him. A fleeting sense of remorse for his betrayal of Dorothy was countered by the thought that they had barely spoken to each other for the past few days: She spent all her time on her bloody frescoes and was too tired at night to do anything much more than sleep. Whereas Eva had made herself available to him more and more readily; she listened sympathetically to his problems and agreed with him that a wife should think of something more than her own concerns: Her husband had needs too. He was a fool, he realised, for having restrained himself so long.

He brought the car to a stop at the side of the road, turned to face her and placed his hand on top of hers. "I understand," he began, but before he could say anything else she had almost thrown herself at him and their bodies were locked tightly together. When they paused for breath, she drew slightly away from him and smiled weakly. "Thank you," she whispered. "You don't know how long I've been waiting for some sign that you cared." He was about to embrace her again, but she pushed him gently away. "Not here. Let's forget about lunch and go back to my place."

"Don't you live with your mother?" he asked, as he turned the car round and set off back to the town.

"No, on my own. My mother's been dead for five years." She seemed to have forgotten all about the chickens and vegetables that had saved her life during the siege, but there seemed little point in reminding her of those now.

"Yes, I *had* noticed that particular detail," Luigi said, "but I don't see why it should upset you so much."

"Neither do I, really. It's just that her other Virgin, over here—the one she must have based on Helena—is so full of love and warmth, so tender and nurturing, all the things you want a mother to be. By contrast this one seems cruel and vicious."

"Just because she shows a woman hitting a child? Almost every child was beaten in her time; it was considered good for them, there was nothing abnormal about it. You have to remember that she *was* a woman of her time, however exceptional, and however much you may want to see her otherwise."

"But don't you think it undermines the positive image of the Virgin?"

"Yes, and I'm sure it's intended to. But that doesn't make Margaret a traitor, as you put it. She might well have felt some justified antagonism towards the sitter—didn't she refer to one of them as a 'simpering harlot'?"

"I don't remember. I think that was someone else." How

strange, she thought: These are exactly the words I would use to apply to Eva, and the more I look at this picture, the more the woman begins to resemble Eva—the same angular face, the curly reddish hair, the air of fake innocence, the false smile.

"Don't you think we should find out where Eva and Roger are?" she blurted out, then stopped in embarrassment, realising that she had made a potentially offensive association.

Luigi seemed not to notice. "I'm sure, wherever they are, they don't need our company," he said quietly, but once again with an undertone of bitterness.

Sensing his hurt, she decided to speak openly about the matter. "I should apologise for Roger," she said. "I don't think he means any harm, but he can't seem to stop himself from—not falling in love, but becoming mildly obsessed with any attractive woman he happens to meet. Usually it doesn't lead to anything very much, but it can cause problems while it lasts."

"Usually?" he repeated.

"Once or twice it has. But I'm sure it's not the case here."

"I wish I could share your confidence. But I know Eva too."

It seemed time to change the subject. "Look," she said, "it's too late to get back to work and I'm pretty muddle-headed after all that wine. Why don't we try to find my parents' house? Have you asked anyone about it yet?"

"I did mention it briefly to my father. He said the only large houses from that period that have survived our various ethnic, religious and political cleansings are all on the same road, towards the outskirts. They were all turned into municipal offices, which is what they remain, so you won't find much there that you recognise. Anyway, they'll all be closed by this time. But the garden might still be there."

"Let's take a taxi and go and look."

• • •

He tried not to show his disappointment, saying the usual things about how wonderful it was, the greatest ever, and so on. In truth, although he felt he had done his best, he had become increasingly irritated at her obvious belief that vigorous athleticism and constant changes of position, combined with a good deal of noise, resulted in ecstatic lovemaking. It was always like this, however: Every new woman seemed a letdown by comparison with Dorothy, who seemed to know exactly what to do to please both him and herself. So what drove him to this futile search for something that could not possibly be better?

"Had you ever tried it that way before?" Eva asked, as they lay side by side smoking.

"No," he replied, truthfully enough. He had seen it illustrated in books, but had never believed it was physically possible.

"You should try it with your wife sometime. It might liven her up a bit."

He resented her intrusion into his private life and also the suggestion that Dorothy might need "livening up," but said nothing.

"She seems very dull to me," she went on. "No interest in anything but her stupid paintings. No wonder she gets on so well with Luigi."

He felt a spasm of self-hatred, realising that it was his own disloyalty that encouraged her to speak in this way.

"We get on all right. I've nothing to complain of."

"I thought you had. Why are you here with me, then?"

"Because you're a beautiful woman and I like you." He tried to kiss her, but she wriggled away and settled down some distance from him. "I thought you felt more than that," she complained. "I don't want to be just some kind of local souvenir, another addition to your list of conquests."

He knew the game she was playing and what his next move was supposed to be, but he rebelled against making it. "Why are *you* here with *me* if you're sleeping with Luigi?"

"'Sleeping' is the word for it. That's about all we do. He's too much of a gentleman for anything else. He thinks the missionary position is a daring perversion."

"Why do you stay with him, then?"

"He's useful," she replied vaguely. Assuming her flirtatious, hurt-little-girl role once more, she pouted encouragingly: "Why are we talking about them, when we could be doing something much more interesting?"

It wasn't all that interesting either, but once again he did his best. "Tell me about your other lover," he suggested, as they lit their next round of cigarettes. "The one in the caves. Romeo."

"His name is Walter. That's not his real name, it's a nom de guerre, but everyone calls him that, including me. He's with the guerrillas."

"So they're not 'terrorists' any longer?"

She took a long draw on her cigarette before replying. "It's much more complicated than you think. The foreign press has got it all wrong, or at least has simplified it too much. There are faults and virtues on both sides."

"I see. So both sides saw their enemies in half?"

She looked at him in surprise. "How do you know about that?"

He told her about the photo, which he had not mentioned before.

"So he puts it on display, does he?" She went on to explain. The victim had been Walter's uncle; the landlord was no direct relation of hers, but a distant and unloved cousin of her moth-

114

er's. Nevertheless, all branches of both families were implicated in the long-lasting feud. "There have been atrocities on both sides, but this was one of the worst. There are centuries of these blood feuds to be avenged, you know. People are patient, they wait their turn for revenge—for generations, if necessary. The hatreds are personal, national, racial, religious. And each settling-up paves the way for the next retaliation. It'll probably never end."

"I know. You said that before." He wondered which side she was really on, and what part she had actually played in the siege. "So what's happening now is just a truce, not a solution?"

"That's right. But while the truce lasts, you've got a chance to see things more objectively. Why don't I take you to the caves and let you meet some of the guerrillas? Once you've talked to them, you won't judge them so harshly. I can get you there easily enough."

"All right. As long as Dorothy agrees to let me go."

"I'm sure she wouldn't even notice you'd left."

Her heart sank as they drove slowly along the street past a series of high walls that obscured the houses behind them almost completely from view. "It's no use," she said finally. "We'll have to get out and walk and try to peer through the gates. Let's ask the taxi driver to wait—I'll pay for his time."

The barred gates offered some glimpse of the buildings behind but none of them sparked the moment of recognition she had hoped for. She began to feel it was hopeless: She remembered a huge house with limitless space around it, completely isolated with no close neighbours, and, if this was so, none of these could be the right one. She had been much too young to have a clear understanding of her surroundings and her memory of them could only be faulty. She was about to give up and apologise to Luigi for wasting his time when she realised that one of the gates was unlocked and invitingly ajar. She gave a tentative push and it swung groaningly open; Luigi nodded as if giving her permission to enter and she stepped inside.

The house was abandoned, its facade cracked and pitted with the impact of shells and bullets, the front door dangling precariously inwards by its bottom hinge and half the roof blown away. All the windows were smashed and, after an attempt to board some of them up, the remainder had been left as they were, framed by jagged fragments of broken glass. The garden was a wilderness of knee-high grass and weeds, tangled and overgrown bushes and a few stunted and decaying fruit trees. Yet she recognised it at once, overcome by a sensation of combined strangeness and familiarity: the yellow two-storey building with the steeply sloping red roof, the irregularly sized and shaped windows, above all the small verandah in the top left-hand corner whose white pillars now gaped at intervals like missing teeth. "We had breakfast up there," she said, pointing. "In summer. And I used to play there, with Mark."

"Who's Mark?"

"My brother. He died."

They made their way to the door and into what was once the hallway, but it was impossible to explore much further: Shells had left gaping holes in the floor and the staircase terminated abruptly after half a dozen steps. "It all looks so diminutive," she said, "without the original furnishings. But everything always seems so much bigger to a child."

They wandered into the garden and stopped in the middle of a patch of half a dozen ruined fruit trees. "What kind do you think they are?" she asked "Apples? Pears? Cherries?"

"I've no idea. I'm no expert. Does it matter?"

"It might." The trees too were much smaller than they should have been, though they could well seem huge to a little child peering up at them. She looked round to see where the bullet might have come from, but the wall seemed to offer adequate protection, unless the sniper had been on a neighbouring rooftop. Perhaps she had imagined the whole shooting; perhaps Mark had just lost his balance and fallen to the ground, smashing his head open. Perhaps Mark had never even existed and she had invented him as an imaginary playmate. But surely that was ridiculous.

"I loved him," she said aloud. "He was always kind to me and looked after me. He was picking a pear for me to eat when it happened—perhaps he just reached over too far and fell. In that case, though, why did my parents never mention him? My mother always avoided my questions about him and said she would tell me later, but she never did. Maybe they blamed themselves for not looking after him better."

Luigi was staring at her in bewilderment. "Sorry," she said, "I'm talking about my brother. I remember him being shot by a sniper as he climbed one of these trees. That's what I *think* I remember anyway. He fell right at my feet. Actually I *did* ask my mother once, when I was a teenager, but all she said was that it was best to put sad memories behind you and forget them. That's all she would say."

She felt she was about to burst into tears, not just from the memory but from the frustration of not being able to articulate it properly or even to be sure what it was that had taken place. Sensing her distress, Luigi put his arms clumsily around her and hugged her. She let him hold her for a moment before gently detaching herself. "I'm all right now, thanks. Whatever happened, there's nothing I can do about it now. Let's go back into town and have a drink. If only you could get a gin and tonic here instead of that awful brandy."

In the taxi they both remained silent until they had almost reached their destination. "They say that memories are composite things," she said suddenly. "They're never totally pure or exact; you put them together from several different incidents and sometimes from what you've been told or read about as much as from what you've actually experienced. That must have been what happened here. Not that it's any comfort, I suppose."

"But you *did* have a brother, didn't you, and he *did* die?"

"I think so. But somehow I feel now that I'll never know."

To her amazement and eternal gratitude, as she quickly assured him, Luigi whispered something to the waiter and slipped a few bank notes into his hand; he returned a few moments later with a full bottle of English gin. "It's their last one," Luigi explained, "and they've been hiding it away for a special occasion. I told him that *you* were a special occasion and he agreed to cooperate. You don't need to drink it all just now— they'll put the rest aside for you for later. The tonic is local, I'm afraid, but it probably won't destroy the gin completely."

She drank it gratefully and he poured her another glass. "You know," she said, "I've never even told Roger about Mark. I know it sounds crazy, but somehow I never got round to it. It's probably because of what happened to Jill, my daughter from my first marriage. She was killed too, in a car accident."

He gave a murmur of sympathy, but she continued hurriedly before he could speak. "Maybe I'll tell you more about it later; there've been enough disasters for one day. Although Roger's been kind about it and has tried to show proper sympathy, he seems to feel that I brood too much over Jill and ought to 'get over it' better. So, if he knew about Mark too, it would be rather like Lady Bracknell—'To lose one child may be regarded as a misfortune; to lose two looks like carelessness."'

She poured herself another drink. "Tell me about Eva," she asked abruptly. "Are you in love with her?"

"I don't know that I would call it love exactly, and I know well enough that she doesn't care much for me. You could call it an obsession if you like, an infatuation. Isn't there an English word 'besotted'? That probably sums it up best. And I know she has other lovers."

"You should find someone else. That's easy to say, I know."

"You don't like her, do you?"

"Not very much. But I hardly know her. Perhaps she has hidden virtues—well hidden. I'm sorry, I don't mean to offend you."

"That's all right. You can't say anything worse about her than I've said to myself already, hundreds of times. It doesn't do any good, though."

She's probably good in bed, she thought, and, as if reading her mind, Luigi went on, shyly averting his eyes: "It's not even as if we make love well together, though I'm sure that's my fault. She always makes me feel it is, anyway."

She wondered if she should offer to console him, but, raising his head, he said it was time to change the subject: His love life—or lack of it—wasn't all that interesting.

"I hope Roger doesn't do anything too stupid," she mused, speaking as much to herself as to him. "Like saying he's fallen in love and is going to stay on here. He's done something like that once already. But he wouldn't want to leave his job, it's much too important for him."

"Is he a good lawyer?"

"Yes. Very good. And an honest one too, which is pretty rare.

119

He's got a strong social conscience and he'll only take on work he really believes in. He makes some compromises, of course—we all do—but he has a lot of professional integrity." She laughed shortly. "It's his private integrity that worries me."

Luigi remained tactfully silent, but she needed to express herself to somebody. "I knew that, after his divorce, he had gone wild for a year or two, but that's common enough. Even when I was going out with him, there were always others around, at least to begin with. I thought that would end when we got married, but it didn't, not really. The only consolation is that it rarely lasts for more than a few weeks, even when he thinks it's deadly serious. But I don't want to make him out to be worse than he is; he has lots of good qualities too. Generally we get along pretty well together."

She fell silent and began to rub her empty glass between the palms of her hands. He made a gesture to refill it, but she waved the bottle away: "That's enough for now and it wouldn't do to drink the only bottle all at once."

"You know," he said, after a pause and clearly trying to change the subject, "these odd ideas that Margaret attributes to Dimitrios about reincarnation and multiple universes—I don't believe them, of course, but there *is* a sense, isn't there, in which our lives are potentially infinite, depending partly on choice, partly on sheer accident. You get up five minutes earlier or later than usual, you miss or catch a bus to work, you meet or don't meet someone as a result—and your whole life is altered. Perhaps irrevocably."

If David had left five minutes earlier or five minutes later, she thought, Jill would still be alive and he and I might still be married. Or no, we would have divorced anyway, but I would still have her. And because we divorced at a different time, I might not have met Roger. And, if I hadn't met Roger, he wouldn't be here to take Eva away from Luigi—though I'm sure she would still find someone else. But then *their* lives might have developed differently as well and we might never have met at all. She shook her head: It's all too complicated, she thought. Maybe Dimitrios was right and there is another universe—other universes—in which all these variations are played out, though none of them may be much improvement on this one.

She realised that Luigi was staring at her, puzzled by her silence. "Time to go," she said. "It's getting late and it's been a tiring day."

As he could think of no way of moving tactfully into the subject, he introduced it directly: "Eva offered to take me up into the mountains one day."

"That's nice. Whatever for?"

He had thought it over and spoke carefully: "She has a friend there, among the guerrillas. She wanted me to meet him and learn something about the other side in the conflict. She says there are faults on both sides."

"I bet she does. When did they become 'guerrillas' rather than 'bandits'?"

"We've just heard one point of view so far. I'm sure there's another one."

"What about her Florence Nightingale act, when she risked her life saving innocent people from these supposed monsters?"

"I'm sure that was genuine enough. Why do you doubt it?"

"No reason. Is this 'friend' what I suspect he is?"

He was about to display indignation, then realised that it might divert suspicion to concede the point: "I think so. Rather like Romeo and Juliet, I gather."

"How romantic. And where does Luigi fit into this touching scenario?"

He offered no response. "Anyway, I'm going," he said.

She thought for a moment. "Don't these terrorists—sorry, guerrillas—live in caves up there?"

"I think so."

"In that case, I might like to go too." She smiled at the look of panic in his eyes.

"Why?"

"I might find some information about Margaret there." She made no attempt to elaborate, knowing that every reference to her work now brought an automatically hostile reaction from him. "And, in any case, I think I need a break, I've been working too hard."

"I thought you were short of time as it is?"

This was true enough, but his obvious reluctance to have her accompany him roused a desire to goad him: "Suppose you get kidnapped and I have to ransom you? I don't have any money and each week they'll send down an ear or a toe or a finger, or perhaps something worse, to remind me that it's time to pay up. No, I can't let you go; it's far too dangerous."

"Don't play games with me. I'll be all right with Eva to look after me. I'll only be away for a day. Perhaps a night too, if we run into any problems."

"I'm sure you will. Run into problems. They must certainly abound up there. Enough for several nights, I'm sure."

He tried to control his anger, knowing his position was weak. "What else do you expect me to do? Hang around here all day, drinking their foul brandy and getting ambushed by Adam at every turn?"

She looked at him directly. "You could always go home, you know. We've been here well over a week and you can see that

122

I'm quite safe. I'll want to stay here as long as possible, which means longer than the three weeks we planned for. You'll be a lot happier at home, working."

He attempted a compromise. "All right. I'll leave in a couple of days. In the meantime, I want to go to the caves."

"Fair enough." It was probably the best she could hope for. Although she would genuinely like to visit the caves herself, she realised that it would almost certainly be a waste of valuable time; if necessary, she could try to fit them in just before she left.

More confident now, he tried to embrace her, but she turned away. "I'm tired." In reality, she had no desire to be his second woman of the day, but there was no point in listening to his denials now.

"Everything's all right," he told her happily. "Dorothy says I can go."

"How gracious of her."

Her sarcasm deflated him. "I would have gone anyway, whether she liked it or not. I said I'd be away a day and a night, but perhaps we can stretch that." He said nothing about his promise to leave afterwards: Perhaps that could be stretched too, or the situation might somehow have resolved itself by then. "When can we go?"

"Not for a day or two, I'm afraid. I have to make contact with Walter and arrange a safe-conduct. And I have to make arrangements for the store while I'm away. In fact, I should be there now and I'd really better go." But she made no move to leave.

"What about this afternoon?" he hinted.

"Sorry. Not possible. Maybe tomorrow."

An empty, dreary day loomed ahead of him. "Isn't there *something* I can do? Anywhere I haven't been already?"

She thought for a moment. "Well, there's the museum itself, the one Luigi works at, not the one you've been to already. But it's really pretty boring, just a lot of old Roman pots and things like that. For some reason, they have a room full of decorated tiles from stoves and chimneys. Some people seem to think that's interesting."

"If I get desperate, I'll go there." He would be sure to run into Luigi, though, and perhaps even Dorothy.

She seemed reluctant to go, despite what she had said. "There's something I should say." She kept her head turned away from him and ran her coffee spoon nervously through her fingers. "What happened yesterday was wonderful, I'll never forget it, but I don't think it should happen again."

"Why not?"

She still avoided looking at him. "You'll be leaving soon, and I'll be staying here. We both know that. It would be terrible if we began to feel too strongly about each other. It's best to leave it the way it is now."

It was impossible to tell how sincere she was and if she was capable of feeling deeply about anyone except herself. He was tempted to call her bluff and tell her not to worry: They should just have a good time together and then forget one another. That was how it would have been anyway.

"There's another reason," and now a tear glistened in her eye as she looked at him. "When we go to the caves, I will have to be with Walter. He's terribly jealous, very possessive. So it would be impossible anyway."

Then why did she suggest it in the first place? he wondered. And why should it bother him? He didn't really care whether he slept with her again or not, and yet, aware as he was of her duplicity, he found himself stretching his hand towards her. "It's all right. I understand. But I *am* disappointed all the same."

"Are you?" She grasped his hand tightly and smiled hazily through her tears. "But I knew you would understand, there's something so special about you. Yet I don't want to hurt you." She turned her head away and dabbed at her eye with a handkerchief in her free hand. "Perhaps I can go to work later," she said. "Maybe just *one* more time wouldn't hurt."

⁘Margaret⁘

I have become reckless, I know, but in a sense, I find their obtuseness a challenge. Why does no one ever *look* at a painting properly? You spend weeks or months of your life slaving at it and they come along and glance at it for ten seconds and murmur "very nice" or "I prefer the one on the other side," and they haven't really *looked* at it at all. And, if they *have* looked, they've seen only what they want to see. I have my own little reputation now, for nice, safe ecclesiastical subjects with a "feminine" touch, and now that they've managed to slot me away into the appropriate niche they're not worried about me anymore and they can begin to ignore me. I should welcome that, I suppose, but at the same time, I find it depressing. More and more I smuggle in what seem to me horribly subversive details and stand back and wait for the explosion, and no one even notices them! I have my defence all worked out, and my rationalisations, usually after consultation with Dimitrios, and I've never even once had to use them. I feel like grabbing the spectators by the arm and dragging them to the painting and pointing and asking, "What do you think about that, then? Doesn't *that* challenge everything you've ever believed in?" And even then, they probably wouldn't understand. It makes me wonder whether it's all worthwhile after all.

Meanwhile I pile up dozens and dozens of sketches for the paintings that I *really* want to do but I'm too much of a coward to present openly. Judith and Holofernes, from what seems years ago now. Susanna and the Elders. The martyrdom of St. Catherine, with details that would make the viewers want to vomit on the spot, rather than saying, "Oh, how pretty! How noble! How uplifting!" Classical subjects, too, like the rape of Lucretia, or the Sabine women—but I know these are truly out of the question. Hundreds of them, perhaps, by now, all with details taken straight from life, for the pace of executions increases week by week, now that the invasion from the north is under way. Spies, traitors, dissenters—or anyone even suspected of these crimes—prisoners of war too poor to pay their ransoms, thieves and murderers and forgers, plus the usual crop of heretics. The forger's end was particularly nasty: They built a raised platform with a hole in the middle and set a fire underneath it and put a huge metal cauldron filled with oil over the hole. Then they built another platform, all round the rim of the cauldron, so that privileged spectators could see exactly what was going on, and got the oil boiling, and then they slowly lowered the victim into the oil from a special pulley. *Very* slowly. I could still hear him screaming long after he was dead. I asked someone why this fate was reserved for forgers and he said that their crime directly affected the economy, destroyed confidence in the state and was detrimental to social order, especially in wartime. It was worse even than heresy.

The people are accustomed to me sketching by now and, though their hostility towards me persists and ugly rumours about my activities continue to circulate, I am protected by the public awareness that I am "the Duke's whore," a reproach hissed at me by the boldest of them as they sidle up to me and then vanish rapidly into the crowd. I work a few of the details into my official paintings—crucifixions (for the thieves, of course, not for Christ himself), a martyrdom of St. Sebastian and so on—so that the authorities won't ask why I am constantly hanging around these executions for no apparent reason. But I always tone them down and make them far less explicit than they should be. The "Holofernes," for example, did double duty—appropriately sanctified—for a head of John the Baptist, with a Salome modelled on one of my least favourite of my fellow nuns, a simpering harlot called Sister Dolores. I also used her for an "Eve" that deliberately exaggerated the image of the "temptress" till it became—as I thought openly ludicrous. Yet no one seemed to notice.

The Duke is away, of course, leading the army against the insurrection in the north, and I haven't seen him for almost a month. A strange kind of affection, even trust, has grown up between us, though I don't delude myself that I mean anything very special to him—apart from his wife, whom he genuinely loves, there are at least five or six other regular mistresses. Yet I feel I can confide in him and—apart from Dimitrios—he is almost the only person to have any genuine feeling for my paintings or to understand them. Even he doesn't spot everything, but he did notice the background to my *Marriage at Cana*, with the bride being sawn in half by her father and her husband, and the priest looking on. I got the idea from a local legend in these parts: A boy and girl from feuding families ran away together and were quickly captured by the girl's family, but not before she had been "dishonoured" and thus rendered unmarriageable. Reputedly, the girl's father and brothers sawed the boy in half, and the girl herself was sent, of course, to a convent.

"It's a bit explicit, isn't it?" he remarked, frowning. "Even crude. I see the autobiographical reference, but I thought you loved your father?"

"I did. Very much. But he was willing to make me marry someone I hated nevertheless."

I wish the Duke would write to me. He promised to do so and said he would get one of his servants to deliver the letter, but there has been nothing so far.

More wisdom from Dimitrios. He had made no mention of his peculiar ideas on reincarnation since our previous conversation, but, watching me at work on my *Last Judgement*, he started off once more. I listened rather abstractedly, for though the hell part of this is easy enough, I am increasingly dissatisfied with all my attempts at paradise, which seem inevitably false and insipid. He had finally worked out, he said, how you could have a universe that continued through eternity and *also* a Last Judgement.

"Tell," I encouraged him absentmindedly, concentrating on a particularly unpleasant detail of a woman being flayed. This had actually happened some months ago, and I can no longer remember the exact reasons for it—the horror of the experience drove everything else out of my mind. It had something to do with marital infidelity, combined with incest, and vague accusations of witchcraft concerning the sickness of a neighbour's cow. Given this last charge, I was surprised that they didn't just carry out the usual burning: Flaying is a tricky, time-consuming business that needs to be performed by an expert if the victim is to remain conscious enough to appreciate fully what is being done to her. They must have hired the right person here, for it seemed to take hours and, like the forger, she stubbornly refused to die quickly, screaming loudly and monotonously until even the more self-righteous members of the audience started to feel uneasy and began to shout to the executioner to finish her off soon.

Dimitrios, for all his virtues, has never really understood how I can experience genuine revulsion at these spectacles, yet sketch them and reproduce them so calmly. I tell him that this results from artistic detachment, emotion recollected in tranquillity: First you feel, then you create—not *without* feeling, of course, but with feeling controlled and directed and made useful. So I can't let my own spontaneous reactions get in the way of the artistic effect I am trying to create. He nods dutifully in agreement, yet I am sure he continues to suspect that I take a secret pleasure in witnessing such pain.

I remembered, did I not, he began somewhat pompously, what he had told me about each of us living through, and becoming, every possible form of life that the universe could offer? I nodded. Obviously, he continued, such a concept offered no scope for time to end and eternity to take its place, for it was eternity that was the constant and time merely an illusion, part of the dream each of us repeatedly lived through, for a few poor years, mistaking it for reality.

Or a few poor centuries, I reminded him, if it's our turn to be a rock, or merely a few poor hours if we're one of your beloved flies.

I was having trouble getting exactly the right texture and colour for the point where the skin separated from the flesh. I had forced myself to approach the body at the end, but I was working with pencil and paper and I felt too sick by then to concentrate properly. If Dimitrios were right, I realised, I would have my turn at being this woman and being flayed, and also at being boiled like the forger, or flogged almost to death like the Gypsies last week, before they were packed off out of town. There were a dozen of them, including a couple of children no more than five years old, and they had been driven south by the fighting in the area where they normally lived. At first they were tolerated; then, as more and more refugees poured into the area, they began to be blamed for all kinds of petty crimes: theft and prostitution to begin with, then armed robbery and rape and murder. As little of this could actually be proved, it was thought salutary to "teach them a lesson" and then expel them. The lesson was certainly very thorough and almost as bad as flaying: The flesh was stripped from their backs by the whipping until you could see the bones. Then they were thrown into carts and driven about five miles away and dumped at the roadside. I heard that both the children were dead by this time and that a few of the adults were unlikely to survive either, but there has to be a scapegoat of some kind, hasn't there, and we got rid of our Jews long ago.

The idea of having to live through all this as well didn't appeal to me much, and I began to hope that Dimitrios was mistaken in his speculations. Meanwhile he was saying something about "multiple universes" that I didn't quite understand, and I had to ask him to repeat himself. He glared at me and said sulkily that, if he was boring me, I should ask him to stop and he would be only too pleased to obey. It was fascinating, I reassured him, but, being a flighty, empty-headed woman, I found it hard to concentrate as forcefully on such weighty matters as a man could.

He scowled at me again, suspecting that I was making fun of him, but condescended to go over it once more. Suppose, he said, that there is not just *one* universe, but an infinity of them? And each of us exists in each of these universes, but in a slightly different way each time. For example, you (he meant me) have blue eyes, don't you? Well, in the universe next to this, you would have brown eyes, and that would be the only difference. And in another one you would have green eyes and red hair. But you would also begin to do slightly different things each time and lead a different kind of life—you might still be an artist and paint the kind of pictures that you do, but without being a nun. In that case even your name would be different, for you had to change it when you took your vows, didn't you? But most other things would be the same. Or you might be neither a nun nor an artist and simply get married and have children. And with *everyone's* lives being different in this way, history would be different too, for all these changes would be cumulative. In one universe the Roman Empire would go on forever, in another it would never have existed at all, and in a third it would have collapsed a thousand years ago.

I found all this rather bewildering and tried to get back to the main point. What about the Last Judgement? I asked him. How would that fit in?

Easy, he responded jubilantly. Don't you see? In one—or more than one of these universes—there *is* a Last Judgement, for infinite possibilities—including the possibility that there *is* no infinity—have to exist. So in one universe at least, instead of our continuing to be eternally reborn, it all finally stops and we go off to heaven or hell instead.

I finally got the purplish effect I wanted and stepped back to examine it. How do you like it? I asked him.

You've not been listening to a word I've said, have you? he said. You think I'm crazy and it's all a great joke?

Not really, I answered. It just occurred to me that we might be living in one of the kindest and most pleasant of these worlds; what would it be like to live in one even worse?

· · ·

The Duke returned to the capital last night and is due to visit here tomorrow. In his honour, yet another forger is to be boiled in oil—after initial success, the campaign is going badly and something needs to be done to restore morale. I hear that the victim is a brother of the man who was executed a few weeks ago and he was actually made to stand on the platform and watch it all happening. What kind of idiocy—or sheer impossible desperation—can have caused him to risk suffering the same fate himself? And how can they expect this to deter others, when he himself was not deterred?

I was discussing this with Dimitrios and also musing over a new subject I want to paint—the killing of Sisera by Jael—when he came up with an idea that profoundly shocked me at first, though I have thought about it since and have begun to view it rather more positively. "Why don't you use your influence with the Duke," he suggested, "to have this forger put to death by having a nail driven through his forehead? That will give you a model for your painting and the man will also have a rather more merciful death."

My first response was that it was impossible, immoral, unthinkable: I had no right to decide the fate of another human being in this way. Only someone totally without sensibility or moral feeling could suggest such a thing.

"Only someone totally without sensibility or moral feeling would boil another human being in oil," he replied. "The man is going to die anyway; why not help him to die quickly and relatively painlessly? One blow in the right place, and it's all over. How long did that last forger take to die—fifteen minutes at least? Suggest it to him, give him a choice and I'm sure the man would bless you."

"But being merciful wouldn't be my *real* reason, would it? If

I didn't want to do this painting, you would never have thought of it."

"What does that matter? No one can have absolutely pure motives about anything. Just be happy that you can speed this man to his inevitable demise and derive some benefit from it yourself."

"It's disgusting. I don't even want to think about it any longer."

"You'll have to watch the execution," he reminded me. "With luck you might even be invited to stand on the platform. If I remember rightly, you didn't particularly enjoy the last one. All that screaming."

"The Duke would never permit it. The law says that forgers *must* be boiled in oil. Even he can't change that. And the crowd wouldn't allow him to."

"The Duke *is* the law; he can do what he wants. And it's not really all that much fun for the crowd: They can't see anything unless they're standing on the platform. It's boring just to hear someone scream for twenty minutes. This way they could actually *see* what was happening. It would be a novelty too; they'd like that."

"I'll think about it, but I'm sure it's impossible."

And now, a few hours later, I am on the verge of suggesting it to the Duke after all. Dimitrios is right: If the man is going to suffer anyway, shouldn't I do what I can to ease this and make it as brief as possible? Only no one must ever know that it is done at my instigation: The worst possible motives would be attributed to me, I would be reviled and accused once more of having people put to death for my own pleasure. No one would understand what really lay behind it. And do I really understand this myself?

If the Duke agrees to have the man killed in this way, I will atone for my bad conscience in the matter by making myself the model for Jael—a raging, murderous harridan, crazed with lust for blood, and not the virtuous, patriotic heroine of the story.

It's over. The man died quickly enough, though hardly peacefully, for he struggled and yelled and cursed and protested and begged for mercy right up to the last moment. He never knew that I was responsible for his reprieve—if that is the right word—only that the Duke mysteriously altered the nature of his sentence, and I doubt if he felt much gratitude to anyone as he died. The crowd was puzzled and obviously disappointed, though a couple of hearty disembowelings of traitors soon restored their good humour. I kept myself discreetly in the background, making a few quick sketches as unobtrusively as possible; the body will be secretly delivered to me tomorrow, so that I can study the face at greater length.

The Duke was surprised at my request and at first refused even to consider it. I forced myself to wheedle and pout and exert the full range of my feminine charms, and finally he gave in, though he warned me severely that this was the first and last time that he would interfere with the course of justice for such a trivial reason. It was one thing to hand over bodies that had been properly disposed of, quite another for me to start laying down my own terms for dispatching them.

I promised—honestly enough—never to ask again, for I still felt sick at the thought of what I had done. I almost felt like retracting my request and letting the execution take its planned course, and then I heard the screams of the last forger once more and reminded myself that almost no death could be worse than that.

The Duke has his own problems too, and my petty concerns pale into insignificance by comparison. After the early victories against the insurgents, the army has been beaten back— with losses, he told me grimly, far greater than he can possibly admit to. The result has been to bring all his enemies out of the hiding places in which they had skulked, waiting to see how the tide of events would flow; he had returned to recruit more soldiers—by force if necessary—and to reactivate old alliances among the neighbouring nobility. We would win in the end, he assured me, but at a far greater cost than he had originally assumed, and leaving behind a lasting legacy of hatred.

I returned to my work in a sombre frame of mind, which was far from lightened by having to witness the executions this morning. Sometimes I wish I was not cursed with this demon that drives me to create, often against my better judgement. How much simpler to be like Sister Helena, with her smiling, half-witted acceptance of everything that happens to her, or even like Dolores, concerned only with getting men to ogle her and go mad with despair at the thought that they can never have her.

✠✠✠ DOROTHY ✠✠✠

I've decided to follow Margaret's example and to start keeping a journal of my own. In some ways, her journal has become mine already: I feel myself coming through again and again— in my choice of words, the slant I give to certain episodes, what I choose to put in, what I leave out. Things I change that are too disturbingly close to home, like the boy climbing the apple tree—in the journal, of course, he was stealing pears. If Dimitrios is one of Margaret's alter egos, perhaps I am becoming another. I know I have been translating freely from the start, but, looking back, I can spot one anachronism after another—"emotion recollected in tranquillity," for example, though that expresses surprisingly well what I think she is talking about.

Another reason for writing this is to work out how I feel about Roger. I see almost nothing of him nowadays, except late in the evening. I work late, have something to eat, usually with Luigi, go back to the hotel. No Roger. He comes in around midnight, sometimes admitting to having been with Eva—a meal, he claims, or a visit to the one surviving cinema, even though it has been showing the same mindlessly violent American movie ever since we arrived. Sometimes he has just been "wandering around"; more recently he has offered the extraordinary excuse that he has been with Adam—"he's not so bad after all," he told me, "once you get to know him." Adam and Eva—quite a combination, which I could do something with if I weren't so exhausted. Here he comes now, reeking of her perfume. You'd think he'd at least have the grace to wash it off first.

After reading Margaret's account of how she came to paint the *Jael and Sisera*, I spent a long time (a good deal more than ten seconds, at any rate) studying it. It's certainly very violent—the half-naked man sprawled on his back, arms outstretched, his face contorted in agony, a huge nail sticking in the middle of his forehead, and blood everywhere. She even included the detail from the Bible story that the nail was so large it pinned him to the ground. And Jael squatting on top of him as if making love, wearing a loose dress that rides up, exposing her thighs, her face twisted in a macabre combination of hatred, joy and self-disgust—that's how I read it, at any rate, knowing the circumstances and her own ambivalent feelings about what she had done. Once again, I have to ask how she got away with it—how did they let her paint this on the walls of a church? Was everything permitted, provided it was an "enemy of God" who was the victim? Luigi suggests that in the political chaos of the time—with the town being besieged and relieved several times over in the course of a couple of years—no one had time or energy to check on what she was doing. By the time they found out, it was too late to do much more than cover them up and hide them from view. It was probably quicker to do that than to waste even more time destroying them.

Poor Luigi! I feel he's falling in love with me, in a droopy, devoted kind of way that is probably more a reaction to his misery over Eva than anything really serious. He deserves something so much better than S.H. (the simpering harlot)—he's kind, intelligent, sensitive, loyal—far too loyal for his own good. All the things Roger isn't, I almost said, but Roger is intelligent and—when he wants to be—sensitive and kind. I don't think I can take much more of this, though—either he leaves, very soon, of his own accord, or I give him an ultimatum.

Apart from that one series of entries, there has been nothing more in Margaret's journal about *Jael* and any subsequent remorse she might have felt. It's as if she got all her feelings out in one go and then tried to forget about it, rather than continue brooding forever.

I finally talked at length to Luigi about David and my first marriage and what happened to Jill. A lot of my friends, and almost all those we had in common, dropped me after the divorce: They blamed me for being hard and vindictive and unforgiving—hadn't David suffered too? It wasn't his fault, no charges were brought against him, he had had "virtually nothing at all" to drink. All the evidence was that it was a genuine accident that was unavoidable. What they didn't know was that, by this stage, Jill was all that was keeping us together: The marriage (like all marriages?) was a mistake, we both knew it and yet neither of us was able to take the initiative to end it. Once Jill was dead, it was easy—it sounds horrible to put it that way, but it's the truth. David was just as relieved to be finished with it as I was.

I told him most of this, not very coherently, and he was sympathetic, as usual. He couldn't really understand, however, why I refused to have another child. For all his genuine enlightenment, he still feels, deep down, that it is a woman's destiny to have children and that it's somehow wrong to get married fully intending not to do so. If ever he and S.H. were to get married, he told me solemnly, he would expect to have many children. I forbore to make the obvious comment on this.

And Roger: Why did I marry him? Loneliness, I suppose, and you take what you can get once you've passed thirty-five. But no, there's more to it than that—he was (is?) idealistic, considerate, kind, thoughtful, intelligent. And also fond of women and attractive to them. I knew that, of course, before we married, and thought I could cope with it—I managed to, for about a year. And then he began to resent my independence, the moderate degree of success I started to have in my work, while his own job—didn't stagnate exactly, but he seemed to be marking time, not advancing quickly enough, not achieving the fame and success he had anticipated. It was then that he started to talk about children, but I always felt the true reason was not that he really wanted them but that it was a way to keep me safely at home—and I had told him from the beginning in any case that I didn't want any more. So I said no. And after that came the silences, the tensions, the quarrels, the reconciliations, the affairs—some more open and blatant than others—the steady drifting apart that this visit has postponed but almost certainly not ended.

But I said nothing of all this to Luigi.

This afternoon, after we had gone through a particularly frustrating bout of trying to decipher Margaret's handwriting—which seems, perhaps deliberately, to become more tiny and unreadable as time goes on—Luigi said he would show me something in the museum. I had glanced round it before. It held the usual assemblage of local artifacts and some quite interesting Roman objects but the real gem of the collection, he informed me (kept in a separate room that I had overlooked), was a selection of richly ornamented tiles that had once decorated the huge stoves that some people still use here in their houses.

They were certainly interesting and sometimes beautiful: scenes of harvesting, wine-making, sheep-shearing; people making music with flutes and harps; cottage interiors; feasting and merry-making; deer-, wolf- and boar-hunting; children skating on frozen ponds and rivers and also simple little stories, probably based on folktales, about animals, witches and lovers. As I was examining one of these, Luigi called me over to him.

"This is the one I really wanted you to see," he told me. "I'd seen it before, of course, but had always assumed it was just a typically scurrilous anticlerical piece. Now I wonder if there's perhaps more to it than that."

There were nine tiles that, laid out in order, appeared to tell a story. 1) A young woman takes her vows as a nun. 2) She prays devoutly. 3) She is seen either drawing or embroidering. 4) She makes violent love to a young monk. 5) She flees from the convent, carrying a child. 6) She buries the child. 7) She is taken before a court. 8) She is walled up in a cave. 9) She is torment-ed in hell.

"A version of Margaret's story?" he suggested. "It matches some of the popular beliefs: the drawing (if that's what it is); the monk, probably Dimitrios; the child; the cave. Usually it's the Duke who is the father and she is imprisoned in the cave rather than being starved to death there, but it's quite close. Or maybe it's just that we're obsessed with Margaret at the moment and see her everywhere."

I was about to agree with this when another group of tiles caught my eye—a local version of the Dick Whittington or George Washington story, it seemed, with a small boy stealing fruit from a pear or apple tree, being chastised for this, setting off on his own to make his fortune, prospering as a rich mer-chant, marrying a beautiful woman of obviously high status, then wearing official robes of some kind and finally dying a pious and exemplary death, mourned by all. And I recognised it at once: It was from the stove that had stood in the corner of our kitchen. I had utterly forgotten it and now it all came back—how I had filled out the details of the story in my own mind, conducting endless variations and elaborations of it, even providing my own names for the characters—the hero, I remembered, was called Joachim, a bizarre name whose very alienness must have attracted me.

I pointed it out to Luigi, who said that the stove had proba-bly been kept by whoever took over our house once my parents left, while the tiles, which had acquired value over the years, had been sold to the museum. So where does that leave me now, I wonder, with yet another source for my "memory"?

FIVE

S he had got the safe-conduct, Eva told Roger: They could leave at any time.

"Maybe I shouldn't go," he said. Things were getting worse and worse with Dorothy; they rarely even spoke and, when they did, it was mostly for her to hint that it was time he left. He had no desire to destroy his marriage completely; once they got back home things would straighten themselves out, as they had always done before.

"You're not frightened, are you? And, if so, of whom?"

"Of course not. It's just that I've been here long enough. I have my work to think about."

"What about me? Surely I'm more important than your work?" There had been no repetition of her suggestion that they should stop being lovers; on the contrary, they seemed to spend most of their time in her apartment and in bed. She was constantly trying to persuade him to stay overnight, but he drew the line at that. It was bad enough coming back each time with increasingly implausible explanations for his lateness, without adding extra difficulties. Eva claimed scornfully that Dorothy wouldn't even notice his absence. Though he knew that this was nonsense, he wondered why she had never challenged him on his activities. She must surely suspect what was going on. Perhaps she preferred to ignore it, for the moment at least, in the hope that things would work out again once they were away from here.

He had found an unexpected alibi in Adam, who had met him, either by accident or design, in the hotel lobby one day. He had somehow learned about the trip to the mountains and that Eva was taking him. "Be careful," Adam warned. "You may end up staying there longer than you expect."

"I thought you were the one who suggested I should go there?"

"Yes, but the situation is different now. There are rumours that the terrorists are preparing for a fresh assault."

When he reported this to Eva she told him that Adam was talking rubbish: Everything was quiet just now and would remain that way for several months. Adam was hostile to her, she explained, because she had rejected a persistent series of advances from him and eventually had to be openly rude to force him to stop. Once again something nagged at his memory: Hadn't she said once that she had never met Adam? He had learned by now to be wary of what she told him about herself and all the men who lusted—vainly, she claimed—after her, and once again he wondered why he allowed himself to be passively led along by her as he did. Yet if he refused now to go to the caves, he would be charged with cowardice. It had become a question of honour to go, and afterwards he would definitely leave.

In the meantime he found it useful to keep in touch with

Adam and spend an hour or so with him each evening; that way he could be at least partially truthful when he told Dorothy later where he had been. The man improved somewhat on acquaintance: He seemed to accept that he had been mistaken in crediting Roger with an excessively morbid interest in torture and executions, and he knew a great deal about the history of the area and was full of fascinating tales and legends. Many of these, to be sure, centred round acts of violence and cruel retribution, but, in their context, they were acceptable enough.

Adam professed surprise that Dorothy never accompanied Roger to these meetings and, now that Roger was determined to visit the caves, that he had no plans to take her with him. "It would be ideal for her," he protested, "to see where Margaret lived for the last few years of her life. Margaret was not her real name, you know. She was originally called Artemisia, but had to change that when she entered the convent."

As usual, Roger had no interest in discussing Margaret and replied simply that Dorothy was too busy and, in any case, from what Adam had said earlier, it could be dangerous.

Adam shrugged. "Perhaps I was wrong. There are always rumours that a new assault is imminent. Perhaps it will be delayed until after you have left. It will certainly come, though. There are too many scores left unsettled." He hoped nevertheless to meet Dorothy again before she left: She was a remarkable woman who should be cherished and admired, far superior to others whose attractions were merely superficial and external.

Roger sensed an implicit criticism here, but the man met his gaze steadily and appeared to have no hidden meaning in what he had said. Perhaps Eva had told the truth after all, and Adam had accosted her and been spurned—though to think this was to acknowledge that it was Eva he referred to as superficial. Struck by what the man had said nevertheless, he cut short his visit to Eva later that evening and returned to the hotel earlier than usual, hoping that Dorothy would display proper gratitude at seeing him so soon. She greeted him with her usual curt indifference, however, and spent most of the night writing up what she claimed was Margaret's journal, though he had begun to suspect that she was keeping one of her own, for she covered it up whenever he entered. He looked for it the next morning, after she had left, but, if it existed, she must have taken it with her. As his gesture of goodwill in returning early had been ignored, he felt himself under no obligation to repeat it.

They could leave the next morning, Eva told him, and they would be away for three days and two nights. There would be a drive of several hours up the narrow winding roads into the mountains; eventually they would be met and escorted to their destination. It sounded somewhat melodramatic, but he would have to be blindfolded for the last stage of the journey, even if he would never be able to identify the terrain. As she had warned, they would have to sleep apart for these two nights, though they could certainly make up for it later. She smiled at him encouragingly.

Now that the decision had to be made, he felt increasingly reluctant to go through with it. For all Dorothy's apparent acceptance of the situation, he sensed that he might be taking an irrevocable step, especially as he had originally assured her that he would be away for only one night. He almost felt tempted to set off for the capital and the airport at once, without explanation to anyone, except a note for Dorothy. Eva would think him a coward, of course, but once he was away from her there was no reason to care for her opinion any longer, and he had no intention of remaining in communication with her once he had gone.

On second thought, he decided it might be better to speak to Dorothy first. He could begin a reconciliation by telling her that he had decided not to go ahead with the visit and that he regretted his (stupid but harmless) infatuation with Eva; he had put his priorities in order at last and hoped that they could get off to a fresh start once she joined him back home.

He excused himself from having lunch with Eva in her apartment, saying that he should inform Dorothy of his impending absence right away. She glanced at him suspiciously, then shrugged and said that if he was that much of a prisoner, he should certainly go and beg for his parole. He resented the insult, but replied only that he would meet her later that evening.

Assuming that he would find Dorothy at the usual restaurant, he set off for there. No doubt Luigi would be there too, but he could ask to speak to Dorothy privately for a few moments. He wondered how Luigi would take the news and if Eva had even warned him about it; she had barely mentioned him in the past few days and had assured Roger that she no longer saw him.

They were sitting together at an outside table, Luigi with his back to him and Dorothy facing him. She was talking intently to Luigi, however, and was at first unaware of Roger's approach; before he was close enough to greet her, she responded to something Luigi said by stretching out her hand and stroking him gently on the arm. Roger stopped short and, as he did so, she glanced up and saw him. Withdrawing her hand, she started to get up and began to say something. Without stopping to listen, he turned abruptly on his heel and walked off. He heard her call his name, but paid no attention.

Eva was not in her apartment but he found her in her shop. "I'm staying the night with you," he told her. "I'll go back to the hotel and get my things."

She called his name once and, when he ignored her, she sat down again. "What happened?" Luigi asked.

"Roger. He saw us and jumped to conclusions."

"About what?"

"What do you think?" She was annoyed at his obtuseness. "He assumes we're having an affair."

"Because we're having lunch together?"

"Because I put my hand on your arm."

He seemed confused. "That doesn't prove anything."

"Not for most normal people it doesn't. But he'll use this as an excuse to justify his own behaviour. I wonder why he turned up here, whether he was spying on us or it was just an accident."

"Why should it matter to him what you do?" He spoke with unaccustomed bitterness. "He doesn't seem to care much for you anyway."

"He does, in his own way. Unfortunately, he tends to express it by being very possessive."

"What will you do now?"

"Nothing. Why should I run after him and beg for forgiveness when I've done nothing to be forgiven for? He can come to me if he wants to talk things over."

"He may not have time. He's leaving for the caves with Eva tomorrow."

"How do you know about that?" She had not yet discussed it with him, hoping that it would never happen.

"I have my sources. Eva is much talked about in town."

"Do you mind?" She put her hand on his arm again and looked into his eyes.

"Why should I mind? Her behaviour is a matter of complete indifference to me now."

She thought for a moment, then laughed abruptly. "Do you know what we should do?" she suggested. "We should go to the caves too. I'd love to see the look on their faces when we turned up there."

"That's impossible, I'm afraid. The caves are heavily guarded. Only certain *favoured*"—he put particular stress on the word— "visitors are allowed to go there."

"I know. It seemed an amusing idea all the same."

⫲Margaret/Dorothy⫲

A double disaster: The Duke—or so rumour has it—has been killed in battle. And I am pregnant. The news (the important news, that is; mine is private and insignificant) has thrown the town into total confusion: People are packing their goods and preparing to flee, expecting an invasion at any moment, but in which direction are they to go? The enemy is already ensconced in the mountains behind the town and has been there for weeks; we can see their fires burning each night, but so far they seem content to stay there, drinking and carousing, occasionally sending patrols out to cut off anyone foolish enough to try to escape along the road by the lakeshore. The men are slaughtered on the spot, of course, and any children under ten; the women and older girls—if we can judge from the screams and sobs that drift down from the hillside during the quieter moments of both day and night—are spared for the amusement of the soldiers. No doubt our temporary immunity should be credited to the distraction this provides, and we can expect an attack once the entertainment begins to pall.

Even an escape across the lake, for those lucky enough to have boats, is no solution. With the Duke's death, and even before this, all central authority has collapsed: Local warlords have carved out their own chunks of territory and demand random and haphazard tribute from anyone careless enough to stray into them. If you have exhausted your stock of ransom—gold, jewels, brandy, glassware, livestock, clocks, clothing, linen—or if the women in your party are too old or too young (though this seldom is a deterrent) or too irremediably ugly; if you admit to belonging to the wrong religion, nationality or even family, you are liable to be swiftly dispatched by a bored slash of a sword or a drunkenly skewed bolt from a crossbow.

My own problem seems trivial by comparison. I can avoid detection for a few more weeks or even months, and by then my situation may be so unimaginably different, for better or—more likely—for worse, that it seems futile to try to anticipate or to plan ahead. To escape thinking about it, I throw myself into my work and begin to take the risks I have shunned so far. No one cares any longer what I paint: The Abbess and most of the nuns have shut themselves up in their cells, praying endlessly to be spared the fate they constantly lament and vividly imagine, emerging only to conduct an increasingly perfunctory round of prayers and services.

Cooking and cleaning are neglected, dust gathers silently in the corridors and rats run unheeded through the chapel, their squeaking mingling with the thin sound of our voices as we meaninglessly chant our responses. (One day soon they *will* be heeded, and hunted down for food, but we have not descended quite to that level as yet.)

I am sure we would all starve, if it were not for Sister Helena: Whether she is just a great deal braver than any of the rest of us or is genuinely ignorant of the danger she faces, she forages tirelessly each day, lining up patiently for the few loaves of bread that the one bakery still functioning will allow us, or grubbing in the fields in the outskirts of the town for whatever stunted carrots and onions she can find. Two days ago she came in with her habit spattered with blood and the bread she clutched in her arms soaked with blood also. When I asked her what had happened, she just beamed and shook her head vaguely, apparently oblivious to her condition, and seemed genuinely astonished when I showed her the stains. I heard later that the army in the hills had obtained a cannon from somewhere and had decided to test it by firing at the bread line, a conspicuous enough target in the otherwise empty streets, killing three people and maiming another half-dozen. Though I attempted to stop her, Helena insisted on going out again yesterday, but this time nothing happened: Perhaps they had only the one cannonball or they are reserving their ammunition for a more sustained assault in due course.

The other surprise, though it pains me to admit it, is Sister Dolores. In my uncharitable way, I had imagined her primping and painting herself in secret, longing for the arrival of our attackers and ready to comfort and console them; instead she has proved herself as resourceful and courageous as Helena—perhaps even more so, for Dolores certainly understands the risks she is taking. For the first few weeks of the siege, we existed largely on eggs erratically produced by a few scrawny hens owned by her mother, and fruit and vegetables from the same source. When the hens stopped laying, they went into the pot themselves and then she began to go into the fields, like Helena, and even into the nearby woods, where there was always the danger of encountering an enemy patrol, returning with an astonishing assortment of plants, herbs, leaves and grasses that looked revolting but could be boiled up into if not tasty, at least nourishing soups and stews. Occasionally she comes back with some fish, obtained— with what enticements or rewards I forbear to inquire—from the few fishermen who still venture, usually at night, out onto the lake.

It is not, I hope, cowardice, that prevents me from accompanying her or Helena and sharing in the dangers that they face. For the moment, they provide adequately for us and I have (or so I tell myself) more important concerns. Each day I work steadily and grimly in the church, ignored by the crowds that flock there to pray for deliverance from the enemy and cluster round my picture of the Madonna, to whom they have begun to attribute miraculous powers. This is not, of course, the painting based on Helena, which remains a sketch—though high on my list to be properly worked up soon—but one of my Christ-in-glory–style compromises, using as a model this time Sister Christina, whose features and demeanour are both neutral and healthy enough to satisfy my multitudinous censors. About two weeks ago, an elderly woman claimed that the Virgin smiled at her as she knelt in prayer before Her, and raised Her right hand in benediction. Since then the poor Lady has been credited with activities that would baffle a professional contortionist—everything short of stepping out of the frame and walking along the nave, though even that cannot be far off now. And each "miracle" has, of course, been attested to by a crowd of witnesses, each competing with the next to claim something increasingly outrageous and farfetched.

I dare not simply find this amusing, however, for there is a real risk that, if their trust in Her to save the town from assault and themselves from massacre seems likely to be betrayed, they will look for a scapegoat—and who better than the creator of the image that has deluded them? At present no one recognises me or associates me with the painting: I am just some mysterious, shrouded figure toiling away at some incomprehensible task in dim candlelight in a dark corner of the building. Even those few who realise that the painting is the work of "the Duke's whore" probably visualise me as some painted and bejewelled wanton, lounging idly in a richly furnished apartment, consuming sweetmeats and sipping rare liqueurs; but my present anonymity would scarcely survive an outpouring of righteous indignation from an enraged mob, and there would be many of my fellow nuns eager to save their own skins by identifying me. In my worst moments, especially since the news of the Duke's death, I envisage even greater terrors: Suppose it is rumoured that His Highness was led astray, weakened, enfeebled, betrayed, in essence murdered by the evil machinations of his witch/whore, and that she is responsible for all the misfortunes that have been suffered? Ah, yes, what then?

Meanwhile I work on a second *Judith and Holofernes*. I already have her displaying the severed head, scowling fiercely and challengingly at the spectator, a variation of my Salome but with some explicit details added. Now I am trying something based on amalgamating sketches I have done at different periods over the past few months. Holofernes (based on Dimitrios as he lay uneasily asleep one day) sprawls untidily on his back, held down by Sister Christina. I myself plunge a sword deep into his throat, thrust right up to the hilt, while my clenched left fist shoves his head to the side and holds it firmly in place. Both of us women are calm, detached, methodical: We are performing a necessary but messy and unpleasant task that we neither enjoy nor shrink from. He thrusts his right arm upwards in a vain attempt to ward off the blow; his legs tense in a final spasm. I lean slightly backwards and away, not in horror at my deed, but in order to get a firmer purchase and manipulate the blade more effectively. I place this painting in the very darkest corner of the church.

Dimitrios finds it there and is suitably appalled. "I never realised you hated me so much," he complains.

"Of course I don't hate you. It's just a painting, nothing personal."

"Hate men, then."

"I don't hate men either. Why should I?"

"Your father, your brothers, the Duke."

"The Abbess, Sister Dolores, Sister Maria. We're all mixed, we all have good and bad in us."

He looked closely at the painting again and shuddered. "When did you sketch me?"

"One afternoon when you were asleep. Snoring loudly."

"I never snore."

"Snoring loudly, as I said. You'd had rather too much to eat and drink for lunch."

"You could have asked my permission."

"I thought you'd welcome being immortalised. Instead of complaining."

"Not immortalised like this." He rubbed the side of his neck anxiously. "I can feel the blade going through me right now."

"That's the whole point, if you'll pardon the pun. To show death as something painful and unpleasant. And difficult too. Not sanitised and aestheticised and distanced into something beautiful."

"There's more to it than that, though. You can't deny that

there's a certain enjoyment there, even vindictiveness. That's how it seems to me, at any rate."

"If that's what you see, then that's what you see. I'm not responsible for your interpretations."

For the first time we were on the verge of quarrelling. Then he shrugged and turned away. A procession was forming in the nave: twenty or thirty people, each carrying a lighted candle. Slowly they approached the Madonna and knelt in a half-circle before her, stretching out their arms in supplication. A babble of anguished pleas, demands, exhortations arose from them: Save our town, heal my baby, give us food, protect my husband/son/father/brother who is fighting to defend our country, smite our enemies, restore the Duke to us, let me walk, let me hear, let me see.

And then, shouts of excitement mingled with terror: She hears us! She smiles kindly upon us! She moves! She is coming among us, to heal and protect us!

And then a sudden roar, a blinding flash of sunlight, as a hole appeared in the roof and a cannonball hurtled down into the very centre of the group.

There is a gap of what must be at least a year before the entries resume, and these are even more fragmentary and elliptical than anything that preceded them. With Luigi's help, I try to reconstruct what must have happened in the interval: the return of the Duke (his death only a rumour after all); the lifting of the siege; wholesale official retribution against the insurgents and the settling of private feuds, leading to the reestablishment of (some kind of) order; the birth of Margaret's child and its unknown fate.

"It was in this period," Luigi said, "while she was still largely unsupervised, the church and political hierarchies both being preoccupied with more important matters, that she must have produced her most scandalous works, transferring them from hidden sketches into full-scale paintings, working against time, knowing that inevitably someone would finally pay attention and call a halt, that there was a strong possibility, almost a certainty even, that they would be destroyed. Jael, Susanna, her unorthodox interpretations of the Virgin, perhaps also her fabled visions of hell must all have dated from this period."

This conversation (or rather, lecture) took place in our usual restaurant haunt, as I continued to make steady inroads into the bottle of Tanqueray—fortunately, it is of the oversized variety supplied to pubs and restaurants and will keep me going for some time yet. Now that Roger and Eva have gone off together, Luigi seems more relaxed, as if he has accepted his rejection and is content, possibly relieved, with it. He has even—in his shy, hesitant, apologetic way—hinted that it might be nice if we were to become lovers, but, though I have become very fond of him, this is not a prospect that interests me much. A week ago I might have considered it, if only to remind Roger that someone, at least, still finds me attractive, but somehow this doesn't seem important any longer. And, in any case, I will be leaving here soon. So I let him hold my hand and occasionally kiss me, but have made it clear that this is where it ends. Perhaps, deep down, I don't really want anyone except Roger to make love to me: When he forgets his insecurities and ambitions and resentments and responds to me fully and openly as a person—not as a testing ground to set against his latest conquest or an obligation to be drearily fulfilled—then I know for certain that I could never want, or be happy with, anyone else.

To avoid thinking of this, I return to our perennial topic: "I can understand why her 'hidden' works no longer survive, but

I wonder why there is no sign of her second *Judith*?" After reading the entry that described it, I had immediately gone back to the church and meticulously examined every corner with the help of a flashlight. At first I thought it must have been plastered over like all the others, and that the plaster, in this case, had failed to come loose under the bombardment, but there was clearly no available space that could accommodate it, unless it was on the opposite wall, now covered with what must be the latest of a whole series of restorations—some dire examples of worse than mediocre eighteenth- and nineteenth-century conventional pietism. According to Luigi, who claimed to have finally plucked up courage to accost his boss on the subject, this work is utterly sacrosanct and can on no account be tampered with: "It satisfies a deeply felt need within the simple people of the town. They turn to it in their hour of need, they even credit it with miraculous properties. Even if work alleged to be by 'your Margaret' *did* exist beneath it, it would doubtless merely perplex and distress them, instead of offering the comfort they require." Luigi had smiled in embarrassment as he reported this, lowering his eyes and shuffling his feet like a naughty schoolboy, but had made no suggestion that we should defy or ignore this ruling.

"I'm going back to the church," I said, finishing off my drink, "to try to find it. I may use some rather unorthodox methods and, if you want to avoid trouble with your boss, you'd better not come with me." He stared at me sadly, but offered no objection.

I found a hammer and chisel, abandoned among the debris left by the halfhearted reconstruction that had been forgotten in favour of more urgent priorities, and set to work in what seemed to me "the very darkest corner" of the church, where any damage to a chubby infant Jesus, smiling inanely as an anorexic Virgin drooled in besotted admiration over him, was unlikely to attract immediate attention. The flaking plaster, however, revealed only a bare wall beneath. I moved a foot or so along and tried again, with the same result. My third attempt, however—on a mournful Christ displaying a Sacred Heart that emitted a veritable fireworks display of coloured lights—exposed what seemed to be an older painting underneath. I looked around guiltily, took a deep breath and hacked away furiously, not daring to pause lest I should lose my initial access of gin-inspired courage and begin to consider the likely consequences of what I was doing. The plaster crumbled, then suddenly fell away in large chunks that hit the floor with such reverberating force, echoing loudly in the utter silence around me, that I stopped in alarm, half expecting the curator himself to rush in, wrapped in his silk bathrobe and panting from the unaccustomed exertion.

The scene, to my surprise, was a garden that seemed at first to be Eden, with a chastely fig-leaved Adam and Eve reclining at the foot of an apple tree. Though competently enough executed, the painting was bland and uninteresting—a "safe" work, if it was indeed by Margaret, and certainly not one that could have aroused hostility and suppression. In for a penny, in for a pound: I hacked away until another large section of plaster clattered to the floor and I realised that I was looking at one of those paintings that combined several different time periods—a whole lifetime even—within the same overall composition. Now the couple had a baby, and Eve/Dolores (for I guessed that she was the model) dandled him on her knee, simpering benignly. The saccharine quality of the picture now began to look suspiciously like satire or parody rather than something to be taken seriously. Hack, hack, and now they have another boy, three or four years old already, an ugly little brute, tormenting some helpless furry animal while his older brother (Cain?) vainly intervenes in an attempt to stop him.

Something is going wrong with the story here, I think, and then whirl round in dismay as I hear a footstep behind me. But it is only Luigi, though he is clearly appalled at the desecration I am committing and makes a vague gesture with his arms as if to stop me.

"The curator," he mumbles despairingly, and "Screw the curator," I respond fiercely, motioning him to stand back as I take another swing. The boys are a few years older now and still their roles are reversed, the younger indulging in mayhem while the older dutifully brings a basket of fruit to his indolent parents as they sprawl under the apple tree locked together in pneumatic bliss. There is another baby too, possibly a girl. Everyone is still naked, I point out to Luigi, and the setting must still be Eden, yet death and cruelty exist here already, and the faces of Adam, Eve and Abel are no longer bland and innocent but twisted and distorted into shudderingly vivid expressions of evil and viciousness. Only Cain appears untouched by the degeneration the others have undergone.

I give the wall another battering and Luigi moans feebly, pleading wordlessly with me to stop. He looks around and even up at the ceiling, as if expecting the curator to abseil down through one of the imperfectly patched holes in the roof and snatch both of us away to perdition. It wasn't hell that she was painting, I realise, but paradise *as* hell: The two exist together, there is no division between them, no age of total innocence we came from or to which we can expect to return. No wonder they were so outraged. And now I reveal the image I have known all along I would find there, set out in sequence like the panels of a comic strip: Cain climbs a fruit tree and stretches out his hand to pick an apple (or a pear); Abel takes aim with a homemade yet fearsomely efficient crossbow; Cain tumbles to the ground, transfixed by an arrow through his forehead, falling right at the feet of his little sister, who gazes at him in silent horror, her mouth open in a never-ending scream.

Six

They drove steadily uphill through the wooded lower slopes of the mountains. The heat was not as oppressive as in the past few days and he savoured the cool breeze that blew through the open windows. His thoughts were uneasy, however: Had he been right to leave without even speaking to Dorothy after that scene in the café? What if he had misinterpreted her behaviour there? Suppose their estrangement continued once they returned home? Suppose she refused to return home? But she would hardly abandon her job on a mere whim of resentment, and she was equally unlikely to give up everything just to be with someone as colourless and anodyne as Luigi.

Sensing his preoccupation but misinterpreting its cause, Eva laid her hand on his arm and snuggled closer to him. "I know what you're thinking about," she whispered. "Dorothy and Luigi. But why worry about *them* when we have each other?" When he made no response, she continued, unable to control totally the malice in her voice, "I just hope he performs better with her than he did with me, that's all."

He gave a snort of disgust and shook her arm away, muttering that he had to concentrate on his driving. The road was becoming quite hazardous now, steep and narrow and poorly surfaced, with alarmingly sharp bends offering little choice between a sheer cliff face on one side and a precipitous plunge into the valley on the other. He slowed down to a crawl, the car labouring under the effort, and wondered what would happen if they met someone coming down, though, under the circumstances, that was highly unlikely.

"Walter loves this drive," she murmured, as if to herself. "He says there's no greater thrill than coming downhill at top speed. He drives almost as fast going up as well."

When he ignored this, she swivelled round in her seat and gazed back into the valley. "You can see everything from here," she informed him, "the town, the lake, the woods. It all looks so peaceful. Why can't it always be that way?"

"I think your friends up here may have something to do with that." He wondered once again what her motives were in latching on to him so tightly: It could hardly be love, however freely she had begun to use the word recently. Could she be hoping that he would divorce Dorothy and marry her instead, giving her a legal right to emigrate from here and live abroad? His partners in the law office had dealt with many similar cases. Surely that was rather farfetched, yet her own country offered few prospects beyond endless years of subdued tension, flaring at intervals into internecine warfare. In the chaos of the last year, local warlords had vigorously carved out their personal fiefdoms and were reluctant to abandon control now that a temporary and uneasy truce had been agreed to. Bands of drunk and drugged freebooters, armed to the teeth, swaggered round huge areas of the countryside, seizing anything that took their fancy—houses, furniture, cars, livestock, women. A semblance of order had been restored in the larger cities, but under the ruthlessly authoritarian control of those who had earlier manipulated the racial and religious hatreds to their own advantage. Piously denounced as war criminals by the rest of the world a few months previously, they were now in the process of being restored to respectability and would soon be making visits to world capitals where they would be honoured as wise and responsible statesmen. He was suddenly aghast at the thought of the risks they had taken in coming here, even if this area was considered "safe" and under U.N. protection, and wondered once again if they would escape unscathed.

In his reverie he had swung perilously close to the edge of the precipice; Eva grabbed the wheel and jerked it round to keep them on track. "You'd better let me drive," she ordered. "Whatever is on your mind, I'm not going to let you kill us because of it." He obeyed meekly, stopping the car and getting out, then began to shiver uncontrollably, whether from awareness of their narrow escape or in reaction to his earlier thoughts or simply in response to the sudden chill as clouds swept across the sun and blotted it out, he could not tell.

"Are you sure you're all right? We can turn back if you're afraid, it's still not too late."

"I'm not afraid. Just a little cold, that's all."

She drove much faster than he had, though not recklessly, presumably being familiar with the road. They began to pass gun emplacements built into the hillside as protection from the bombing threatened by the U.N. but never carried out. The men guarding these signalled imperiously for them to stop but, recognising Eva, waved them on immediately.

"You seem to be well known here," he commented.

"Why not? Some of these men were my neighbours a year ago."

He wondered when it would be time for him to be blind-folded and for the promised escort to their destination, but she seemed to have forgotten totally about this and, after passing through a couple of pro forma checkpoints, they reached what must be the main encampment, perched right on top of the mountain, an untidy straggle of tents and hastily erected huts, mixed haphazardly together. "I thought you said they lived in caves?" he remarked, as he squeezed stiffly out of the narrow front seat of the car and massaged his cramped thighs.

"They did, during the fighting. The caves are further down the hill, off the road to the right. We passed them on the way."

A couple of men in nondescript uniform approached them, greeting Eva as a familiar and accustomed visitor.

"They say that Walter is off on business somewhere. He'll be back shortly. Meanwhile, do you want some coffee?" He nodded.

"If you need anything else, the latrines are over there on the right. It's pretty rough-and-ready here. And don't be surprised if you find some women sharing them with you. We're all equal here, all comrades."

He grunted in acquiescence and looked curiously around as Eva began an animated conversation with a group that had gathered round her. As none of those involved showed much interest in him and Eva made no attempt to introduce him, he wandered off towards the edge of the plateau and gazed at the scene beneath. Part of the town was visible, and most of the lake, with some tiny specks that were no doubt farmers work-ing in the fields on the opposite shore. There was no artillery up here, he noticed; it was probably all positioned lower down the slopes, in closer range to its targets. Nothing very much seemed to be happening: Women were preparing a meal while the men lounged around smoking, talking and drinking. One of the larger, more solidly constructed buildings, with iron bars on its windows, had a couple of guards posted outside it who glared at him suspiciously and fingered their rifles as he walked past. He thought he detected a subdued sound of moaning and sobbing from within, but the hostility of the guards deterred him from attempting to investigate more closely. Another smaller and windowless hut also had a guard outside it; here too it was made clear that any curiosity was unwelcome.

A jeep roared into the encampment, driven by a burly, unshaven man in his mid-thirties wearing camouflage uniform, and shuddered to a halt with a squeal of brakes. The man, obviously Walter, embraced Eva warmly and, as Roger approached, she introduced him. Walter offered a quick handshake, then turned away to give instructions or a report to his men. Already prepared to be jealous, Roger felt slighted as well: Why had Eva brought him all this way just to be ignored?

His arm round Eva's shoulders, Walter turned back to him: "Well, how do you like our little setup?" he inquired, in precise but halting English, and, without waiting for a reply, "Throw away that terrible coffee and have a proper drink."

He led the way to a group of soldiers who were passing around a bottle of brandy, appropriated it and offered it to Roger. He wondered whether to wipe the rim, realised that this could be interpreted as an insult and took a swallow, almost choking on a liquid even more raw and searing than any he had sampled in town. "Strong, isn't it," Walter grunted approvingly, before tilting the bottle to his lips and almost draining it. He passed it on to Eva, who seemed to have decided that it was time to discard her habitual refinement and delicacy and adopt the rough-and-ready guerrilla style she had spoken of earlier. She finished the bottle in a single swallow and tossed it casually aside. "Now we eat," Walter continued, moving on to a camp fire over which a pot of stew was bubbling and motioning to one of the women to serve them. Despite Eva's claims of sexual equality in the camp, it seemed to Roger that, apart from Eva herself and a couple of women in uniform, the roles allotted were traditionally domestic.

The stew, made of beans and some unidentifiable meat, was tasty and filling, and Roger ate heartily. Walter spoke volubly and in increasingly imperfect English, occasionally asking Eva to translate for him. He talked about age-old enmities; the injustices suffered by him and his comrades and their families, stretching back for generations; the atrocities committed by the other side, which were never punished or condemned by the outside world; the courage, fighting skills and resourcefulness of his soldiers; their patience and endurance; their love of home and children; the time—now almost upon them—when they would reclaim their rightful inheritance and restore peace and justice to the land. Roger listened despondently, knowing that there was no point in arguing or objecting, for anything he said would be brushed aside as the ignorance or prejudice of an uninformed outsider; even worse was the realisation that he would hear exactly the same arguments, word for word, from someone on the opposite side.

He finished his second helping, mopping up the gravy with a hunk of coarse bread. Walter offered him more, and he shook his head: "It was wonderful, though."

"Do you know what it was? What you were eating?"

"Beef?" Roger suggested, and then, as Walter shook his head, smiling broadly, "Pork? Rabbit? Game? It was good, whatever it was."

"Dog!" Walter shouted, bursting into a roar of laughter that was dutifully shared by his doubtless uncomprehending men. "You have been eating a mangy dog!"

Roger felt as if he was about to gag, then realised that Eva was staring at him and shaking her head slightly. "Don't tease him," she said to Walter. "He doesn't understand your humour yet. Of course it wasn't dog."

When Walter seemed about to contradict her, she gave that almost imperceptible shake of the head once more and, after a moment's hesitation, he clapped Roger heartily on the shoulder and gave another roar of laughter. "Just joking," he assured him. "No dog. We're not under siege here."

Roger smiled weakly back, but the good taste of the meat had vanished and he knew he would never be quite certain as to which of them was telling him the truth.

"Well, what do you think?" Eva asked an hour or two later, when he had finally managed to get her alone. "Do you feel you understand the situation better now?"

"Not at all. It's the same old self-justifying litany of hatred and victimisation, coming from the attackers this time rather than the defenders. I should have expected that, however."

"Why do you say 'attackers'? I told you many of these men lived in the town until a few months ago, when they were forced out. They are just trying to reclaim what is theirs by right."

He shook his head. "I'll never understand it, and I don't think I even want to try. Perhaps I should leave. I've seen all I need to see."

"You can't leave so soon. It would be insulting. You are a guest here. And besides, *I* want to stay."

He decided to change the subject. "What's in that hut over there? The large one, with the guards?"

"The families of some of the men. They are staying there for safety."

"They don't seem very happy; I thought I heard them weeping and sobbing. And why do they need guards, and iron bars on the windows?"

"They have suffered a good deal. They have lost their homes, possessions, families. Everything they valued. Some of them are slightly deranged from the experience. They need to be protected for their own good." She smiled at him beguilingly. He knew that she was lying, but realised that he was powerless to object or intervene.

"And the smaller hut? The one without windows. Also guarded."

"Ah, that one contains a friend of yours." She paused to enjoy his bewilderment. "The landlord of your hotel."

"What's he doing here?"

"It's complicated. I'll explain later. I told you, though, that he was one of those responsible for the death of Walter's uncle. They are going to deal with him."

"What do you mean 'deal with him'? Kill him?"

She smiled enigmatically. "You'll see. It's nothing for you to worry about, however."

He noticed that a couple of soldiers were approaching the large hut. They nodded amiably to the guards and stepped inside. A moment later there was a scream and the sound of a blow; another scream followed, and then silence.

"What the hell is going on?" He moved involuntarily towards the hut.

Eva detained him, grasping his arm firmly. She smiled again, but this time there was a hard glint in her eyes. "Nothing to worry about," she repeated. "Nothing to do with you. Just visiting their families."

Later, he told her he wanted to see the caves. After setting him right on the realities of the political situation, Walter had lost interest in him and was busy planning something with those few of his men who were not by now sprawled drunkenly on the ground and snoring lustily. Eva agreed reluctantly, warning him repeatedly that there was nothing to see there now, except the litter and debris of the previous occupation. When he persisted, she led the way back down the road and then off on a narrow, half-overgrown path where creepers and roots tangled themselves round their feet and insects swarmed in clouds, totally undeterred by his frantic slapping and arm-waving. They seemed to be attracted exclusively to him, he noted bitterly, leaving Eva quite unmolested, as had always been the case with Dorothy at home. Once or twice she used his discomfort as an excuse for suggesting that they turn back; suspecting some ulterior motive, he insisted on continuing.

When they arrived, however, there was obviously nothing to conceal or keep secret. The caves rose in several tiers in the sheer cliff face, connected by a rickety and dangerous-looking series of rope ladders and wooden steps, platforms and bridges. The narrow plateau before them provided a good view of the town and of all possible avenues of approach. Although it was obviously a good defensive position, it could also easily be blockaded, though he seemed to remember Adam telling him that a hidden network of tunnels not only connected the caves inside but allowed secret exits into the wooded area around.

"Well, are you satisfied? Or do you want to go inside?" Her tone was less challenging than indifferent, though, as he gazed nervously at the ramshackle structure above him, she added, in what he took to be a taunting manner, that it was probably too risky for him to attempt to reach any of the higher caves and he should content himself with those at ground level.

"I'll give it a try," he said, irritated at her condescension. "It can't be too bad if people were living here just a month or two ago." He set his foot on the lowest step of the first series of stairs, which immediately began to sway alarmingly, banging against the rock face. It was connected to the cliff, he belatedly realised, only by a random series of iron bolts and staples, many of which appeared to be loose or to have detached themselves complete- ly from the surface. He paused, then, sensing rather than seeing a smile of contempt on her face, scrambled rapidly upwards, trying to ignore the sickening sensation as the stair creaked and heaved beneath him, clutching desperately at the rope bannis- ter that provided a frail and illusory sense of security. He imag- ined himself hurtling against it and through it, bouncing once on the ground and then rolling helplessly over the edge of the cliff and endlessly downwards, his face contorted, his mouth open in a silent scream of terror.

He reached the first platform and paused there, quivering and gasping for breath. "Are you all right?" Eva called up to him, a note of genuine concern in her voice. "It looks far too dan- gerous. Come back down."

"It's all right," he replied, hardly able to believe what he was saying. "I think I'm getting the hang of it. I'll just go up to the next level and look around there." He walked cautiously along the unsteady platform, past a couple of entrances, wishing that he had the sense to admit his fear, content himself with looking inside these and return. The next ascent was even worse, a rope ladder this time, which hung totally loose and swung even more terrifyingly than the stairs he had just left. As he inched his way upwards, grasping tightly to each rung, increasingly reluctant to release his hold and grab for the next one, he made the additional mistake of looking downwards: The whole landscape danced and gyrated in a frantic blur beneath him and he felt he was about to lose his hold completely and topple down. Terror gave him the impetus to scrabble up the last few feet, where he sprawled face down on the platform, panting heavily, oblivious to appearances and to any residual sense of dignity.

"Are you all right?" Her voice reached him more faintly this time and there was no mistaking her anxiety. "Do you want me to go and get help?" The prospect of utter humiliation, as Walter and his men were summoned to his rescue, jeering at him openly, gave him strength once more.

"No, no," he shouted, desperate to deter her before she took matters into her own hands. "I'll be all right now. I'll just look into the nearest cave and come back down." He forced himself to his knees and then to his feet and walked unsteadily to the entrance, firmly averting his eyes from the edge of the platform and the scene below. He paused, trying to adjust his eyes to the darkness that concealed the interior: Why had he not thought of bringing a flashlight or at least some matches with him? This whole business was becoming a total fiasco.

He edged his way a few feet inside and paused again. The light seemed better now and he could see the walls around him, though the back of the cave was still shrouded in complete blackness. He suddenly remembered that he had his cigarette lighter with him and pulled it from his pocket. The leaping flame sent shadows scurrying round the walls, but there was nothing else to be seen, not even the rubbish and detritus that Eva had promised. He heard her voice again, almost sobbing now, pleading with him to return, and he went back to the entrance to reassure her: "Everything's all right. Nothing to worry about. I just want to look round for a moment." Ignoring her protests, he moved back into the cave.

It extended far further than he had expected and, after a few minutes, he began to suspect that he had wandered into one of the connecting tunnels by mistake. The lighter revealed an area only a foot or two around him and he felt a sudden surge of panic, imagining himself lost and wandering helplessly here till he collapsed and died of starvation. Whirling round, he saw the gleam of light from the entrance, smaller now but still reassuringly close; he also heard Eva wailing his name once more and felt a grim satisfaction at her distress: Her concern was doubtless less for him than for the explanations she would have to give if he was injured or even killed.

"It's all right," he yelled, his voice booming and echoing from the walls around him. "I'll be back in a moment." He pushed on, taking care now to keep his hand firmly against the wall to his right so that he could always be sure of finding his way back. There was still nothing to see, however, and it was now merely a perverse delight in alarming Eva and repaying her for her earlier neglect and her scornful remarks that kept him going. The flame from the lighter began to flicker and threatened to go out completely; when he looked back he saw only darkness and the entrance light had vanished completely. It was obviously time to go back but, just as he began to turn, the light flashed over something drawn or painted on the wall. He bent forward to examine it more closely: One of the guerrillas must have been whiling away the time by scrawling graffiti here, a picture of himself and his girlfriend, both totally nude, standing and smiling at each other. It had obviously been hastily composed, for the paint was flaking away already, and much of the picture consisted merely of blotches of red and black, with empty spaces where the surface had crumbled away completely. Yet the faces conveyed a strange and powerful sense of total innocence, of joy and fulfillment, which he would have liked to examine more closely. Now, however, the flame gave a last, sudden gasp and extinguished itself completely, leaving him to grope his way back in pitch darkness, fearful of losing his way till a gleam of sunlight ahead offered assurance of safety.

He emerged onto the platform, blinking, concerned lest Eva had panicked completely and rushed off for help; but she was still there and gave a little scream of relief when she saw him. She began to scold him affectionately as he clambered down the ladder, forcing himself to maintain a facade of self-control, and embraced him tenderly when he finally reached the ground.

"I was *so* worried," she breathed gently in his ear, "so frightened you might fall and hurt yourself. I never imagined you could be so brave." She drew him closer to her and then down on the ground beside her, and began to unbutton his shirt. "You know I have to be with Walter tonight," she whispered. "I can't get out of it. But that doesn't mean we don't have just now."

⁂ DOROTHY ⁂

"It's perfectly simple," I explained to him as I upended the gin bottle and watched the last remnants of the liquid trickle into my glass. I was drinking it neat by now and had waved away all Luigi's offers of diluting it. "Obviously, I was taken to that church by my parents when I was little, and for some reason that part of the wall hadn't been covered up yet and I was wandering around and I saw that painting and it made such an impression on me that I incorporated it into my private fantasies and maybe even invented a brother who got killed in that way. Or maybe I did have a brother and he died of smallpox or something and, for reasons best known to themselves, my parents never wanted to talk about him. I don't suppose I'll ever know."

I knew that I was talking nonsense and that the top layer of paintings that I had destroyed dated from at least the early nineteenth century, but I was desperate to find some rational explanation for what I had seen. I tried out other possibilities: Perhaps the painting had been revealed as a result of some bombardment during my childhood and then covered up again in a deliberate imitation of the overall style of the rest of the wall— anything to avoid the obvious insanity of the other explanations that plucked incessantly at my mind. Luigi, still brooding over what would happen if his boss discovered the devastation I had carried out, scarcely even heard me, and finally I said good night and made my way unsteadily back to the hotel.

There I encountered Adam, waiting for me in the bar, and, if what he told me is true, my own minor vandalism is simply a prelude to what is in store for the town and the church in the near future. "Something is afoot in the mountains," he informed me solemnly, and told me to make preparations for a swift departure. When I asked what evidence he had for this, he said that "strange things" were happening and some people had mysteriously disappeared—the owner of the hotel, for one. I realised that I hadn't seen the man for some time—though that was no great loss—and asked why that was significant. He went into some long and involved story about local feuds and their interminable ramifications, saying that he had been prompted to conduct an investigation by Roger's interest in the photograph the landlord had put in our room. It depicted a commonplace enough atrocity, but he had uncovered links that tied the landlord together with the guerrilla leader who was also Eva's lover. He suspected that the landlord had been kidnapped as part of an ongoing vendetta that could spark off a general resumption of hostilities.

When I expressed concern about Roger's safety, he assured me that he was unlikely to be in any danger. "We are careful here not to harm foreigners," he explained bitterly. "As long as we limit ourselves to killing, torturing, raping and dispossessing one another, the outside world is happy to leave us alone. They will probably send him back down here before any real trouble begins."

I asked if it would be possible to communicate with Roger, but he shook his head. "The situation is too uncertain, but I am sure, however, that he will be all right. I expect you will see him back here tonight or tomorrow." I had to be content with this. However resentful I feel about Roger and his conduct, I would take no satisfaction if he came to any real harm—though a good fright might be a different matter. . . .

But do I even *want* him back, I ask myself as I prepare for my lonely bed, after all he has done? No doubt he'll be all repentant as usual and promise to reform, but perhaps it's time to stop believing him. I've been *so* understanding and forgiving in the past, and all that happens is that he feels he has carte blanche to do it all again.

As for Eva, she's no doubt had her fun and will drift back to Luigi if she feels he can still be of any use to her. And, despite his facade of indifference, he would probably take her, for I think he's really quite shattered by her desertion. In any case, it's time for me to leave and Roger can sort himself out in any way he wants—that's how I feel about it now as I descend into gin-induced oblivion.

• • •

I hold to this decision when I wake this morning. I would like (perhaps) to explore the hell/paradise painting further, but not just at present, for I doubt if I could cope with any more unsettling surprises. I need time to digest it all and, anyway, Luigi seems so terrified by what I have done already that I am sure he would never allow it. Apart from that, my work here is virtually completed. I have photographed and written down descriptions of the paintings and have copied everything that seems relevant from the diaries. The most difficult part is what remains of her journals after the siege. Here the handwriting becomes steadily more indecipherable and illegible, until finally it becomes clear that she is using some code or shorthand of her own that I have no means of understanding. The entries that I *can* read are shorter, fragmentary, elusive, more like reminders or notes to herself than coherent accounts. The overall impression is sad, even pathetic: She seems a defeated woman, her earlier resilience and vitality almost completely gone. Her enemies are gathering round her, the Duke seems to have lost interest in her and offers only nominal protection. She knows it is only a matter of time before he abandons her totally. She is shunned and sworn at when she ventures into the streets; women cross themselves when they see her and men offer crude insults and invitations. She is called a witch, a heretic, a whore, a blasphemer, a murderess; the Abbess gives her the most demeaning and degrading tasks to do, and she carries them out without complaint. What is saddest of all is that she records all this without comment or objection, as if she deserves it and is performing a justified and necessary penance in recording it. Dimitrios (if he ever existed) appears to have vanished, leaving her without any external source of comfort or support, or even someone to test her wits against. There is no mention of any painting; she seems to live in a limbo in which her work still exists and can be seen, however much it is excoriated and reviled, yet she knows that it is only a matter of time before the Duke dies or disowns her and it will be destroyed. At times she seems even to welcome this, as though it will release her from a burden of sin that weighs more and more heavily on her; this impression is strongest shortly before the writing gives way to the impenetrable secret code, and Luigi and I disagree on what these final sections might contain. He thinks that it is a confession, a pouring out of her heart to God and a plea for forgiveness. If that is the case, I respond, why conceal her repentance from the eyes of the world that has judged her so harshly? On the contrary, she must surely have recovered something of her old defiance and sense of self-worth—only something subversive of that kind would require concealment.

The most coherent passages are written soon after the birth of her daughter. The Abbess, it seems, wanted to throw her into the street as soon as her pregnancy became evident, but the Duke had just reappeared, the rebellion was on the verge of being crushed and a spirit of magnanimity reigned for a brief moment. The Duke sent her off somewhere into the countryside for the birth, with orders to leave the child to be brought up there; she apparently obtained permission to visit regularly for the first few months, then the Duke's attention was diverted elsewhere and the inevitable harassment by the church authorities began. Her visits were increasingly restricted in length and frequency; finally they were forbidden altogether. By this time, the child must have been about a year old.

All this is clear enough, and her love and devotion to her daughter emerge even from the briefest and most cryptic of the entries. After that, things become more puzzling and I have to guess, interpret, imagine, fill in gaps and make assumptions in order for any kind of pattern to emerge. She defies the restrictions, slipping out secretly at night to visit the child, or arranging for her to be brought to a place nearby where she might see her. Inevitably she is discovered and punished—first by confinement and the imposition of endless penances, then, scandalously, by being whipped. Or is this reference to "scourging" simply a metaphor, an allusion to her inner suffering and pain? I argued the point with Luigi. He sees it as symbolic, not literal, insisting that physical punishment of this kind would be unprecedented, but I am not so sure. She was totally at the mercy of those who wished to harm her: Why should they observe any restraints?

Then the child dies. How? When? At whose hands? Is she murdered or is the death caused by illness or accident? Here any coherence vanishes and all clues are contradictory. Margaret appears to undergo a period of near-madness. The Duke, the Abbess, the Bishop are variously accused of ordering or committing the crime. She blames the foster parents for neglect, she wildly reproaches herself for her (surely unavoidable?) absence, her failure to protect her child. She imagines an alternative outcome: full defiance of the power of church and state, refusing to give up the child, fleeing with her to another territory, living together peacefully and happily to a contented old age. At one moment she writes as though she had actually done this, the next she rails against the lack of boldness, the weak subservience to the whims of authority that prevented her from doing so. Luigi offered another alternative: a rumour, no better substantiated than any of the others, that the child did indeed survive, that Margaret was falsely informed of her death and she was taken away to be brought up by a noble family who knew only that she had been fathered by the Duke. (If Dimitrios is right, of course, *all* of these things could have happened, depending on which version of her life—or lives—you are examining. Perhaps there is no final or definite conclusion to any life.)

Then follows a more general outburst of repentance and self-abasement, fragmentary and incoherent, and finally, just before the code replaces those scraps of handwriting that I am barely able to decipher, comes a sudden return to lucidity and clarity. The Duke is on his deathbed, she writes, victim of a war wound that had failed to heal properly, and his survival can be only a matter of a few days. He expresses a desire to see her and, grudgingly, the authorities agree. In the presence of his son and heir and of the Bishop and other church authorities, he orders that Margaret's paintings should not be destroyed, but that they should be covered by a false wall and other, more acceptable works should be painted on this. Reluctantly they agree, though it is already too late to save some that have been defaced or irreparably damaged (including, I speculate, the *Death of Holofernes?*). He asks to see her alone. They both have many sins to atone for, he tells her, but his weigh the heaviest. He can try to make his peace with God, but he wishes her forgiveness too: The preservation but concealment of her work is his attempt to satisfy and do justice to both. She has an idea, she tells him, for another painting, a final one (though she doubts she will ever be allowed to execute it), one that will show him there is nothing to forgive. It will be a scene of paradise, of Adam and Eve *after*—not before—the Fall, yet still innocent, still happy and joyful, and she will use the two of them as models.

Did she really mean this, or was she simply trying to console him? And which was her last word on the subject—the painting I discovered yesterday or the vision that she promises here?

· · ·

As it turned out, I didn't have much choice about leaving. A U.N. patrol arrived around noon, and the officer in charge—a ramrod-straight, polite and unsmiling Nigerian, an obvious credit to Sandhurst and the British Empire—told me that I had an hour to pack and that they would escort me back to the capital. We had, of course, registered with the U.N. when we arrived and were apparently the only foreign civilians around, apart from a few stray journalists. There were unmistakable indications, he told me, that all four sides in the interminable conflict were preparing for a renewal of hostilities, and our lives could be at risk if we stayed.

I asked about Roger and whether it would be possible to rescue him too. The officer was astonished to discover where he was and called him a "damned fool" for breaking the agreement we had both made to stay within the town and its immediate environs. There was no question, he informed me brusquely, of endangering the lives of soldiers in order to help people who had disobeyed orders and created their own problems. Aware of my alarm, he softened enough to concede that Roger would probably be safe enough if—as I said he had planned to—he returned today, and, as an even greater concession, he agreed to leave one vehicle and four soldiers till mid-afternoon, so that they could escort him if he turned up by then. After that, however, he was on his own. Whatever else happened, he considered himself responsible for *my* safety, and I had to return with him and the other soldiers within the hour—he would make me accompany him by force if necessary. He's an officer and gentleman of the old school is this major.

Thanks to Adam's warnings, I had packed almost everything already, both for Roger and me, and I needed only a few minutes to deal with the rest. I had looked for Luigi at ten, as usual, but he was nowhere to be found, not even at home, where I encountered a disapproving mother who obviously suspected me of cradle-snatching. Acting on a hunch, I now took a taxi to the ruined house and garden and found him there, gazing thoughtfully at one of the fruit trees. "If you pruned this a bit," he said, as if continuing a conversation we had begun only minutes previously, "and let it grow properly, it could easily be the tree in the painting. And," with a sweep of his hand, "the wall here could be the wall that surrounds Eden."

Despite his distress, he had obviously taken in more of the painting than I had realised, or had perhaps even gone back to look at it on his own. "All trees look alike," I told him, "and so do most walls. Let's not make things more complicated than they are already."

"Don't you want to uncover the secrets of the universe?"

"Not just at present, and I'm sure there's a perfectly simple explanation. In any case, I have to leave." I told him about the major and his ultimatum.

I took a last look at the garden and the house. My parents would sit on the verandah on summer mornings to eat their breakfast. They would send Mark to pick fruit for them, ripe from the tree, and I would tag along behind him like a faithful dog. That had happened, I was sure of it, and, for a moment, I saw them there, standing on the balcony, waving. Luigi was at the gate, waiting for me, and I closed it firmly behind me.

We drove back in silence to the hotel. "I'll write," he promised, as we said goodbye, "and perhaps you'll be able to come back again soon. All these rumours of renewed conflict could well be false, they've happened before. I'll let you know if I discover anything else of interest—perhaps some more of that wall might fall down of its own accord, or it might even get a little encouragement."

The journey took about four hours, with frequent stops at

checkpoints where the major conferred with other officers, and various (to me) incomprehensible orders were issued. Otherwise everything went smoothly: No one fired at us, we hit no land mines, we saw nothing at all apart from the ravaged landscape and some burnt-out villages where ragged children halted their scavenging among the ruins for a moment to stare at us intently, wave or throw rocks at our jeep. I was taken to the hotel where Roger and I had stayed when we passed through three weeks ago, still not fully rebuilt but at least with running water and most amenities.

It is nine o'clock now, and still no sign of Roger. The major had told his men to leave no later than four, so that they would be in good time to arrive here before dark; assuming that they had no more problems than we did, he should certainly be here by now. I suppose I should find the major and ask whether his men have returned on their own, but surely he would have told me if they had. It's not Roger that I'm really thinking about at present, however, but Margaret and her vision of paradise-as-hell and what I might have found if I'd had the time or—let's be honest—the courage to stay on and investigate further. Now that it's too late to go back, of course, that's what I want to do. And so I sit and pour myself another brandy—no gin here, unfortunately, and no obliging boss to pay for it—and listen for the sound of a jeep drawing up outside to bring my own ambiguous salvation.

SEVEN

H e pushed her away and scrambled to his feet, buttoning
up his shirt. "What's wrong?" she asked in puzzlement.
"No one can see us here."

"It's not that." He tried to think of something that would not
hurt her feelings too much, something less blunt than that he
didn't want to be the hors d'oeuvres before the main course with
Walter. "I can't do it knowing that afterwards, in a couple of
hours . . ." He left the sentence unfinished, expecting her to
fawn all over him, billing and cooing that it was he, Roger, who
she really wanted, and knowing that it would make it easier to
resist her if she did. But she simply stood up and brushed the
dirt briskly from her skirt. "If that's how you feel, there's nothing I can do about it. You know what the situation is, you were
fully aware of it when you agreed to come."

They walked back to the camp in silence. When they arrived,
she left him, still without a word, and went off to talk to Walter. He sat around smoking, occasionally drinking the brandy

the men insistently offered him, but barred from further communication by his lack of knowledge of the language and their apparently total ignorance of English. They had another meal, with Walter making more jokes about the allegedly repulsive contents of the stew, to which Roger responded weakly and without enthusiasm. Finally Walter abandoned his attempts to entertain and said it was time for bed: "Eva is in my tent, of course. You can share any one of the others that you wish." He wondered if Walter knew or suspected anything of his association with Eva, but he was too tired and drunk to think clearly any longer, or to care.

He left the tent after the first sleepless hour, sickened by the stench of unwashed bodies, the clouds of cheap tobacco that filled the air, the drunken laughter and singing, the clink of bottles and the vomiting, and spent the rest of the night stretched out on a blanket on the bare ground. The air was warm and the stars shone brightly overhead; he tried to identify the constellations, which he had been able to do without difficulty in his youth, but years of city living had dulled the earlier familiarity and he soon abandoned the attempt. Gradually the singing and laughter and yelling died away, yet he still found it difficult to sleep. He tried to guess which tent belonged to Walter, what he and Eva were doing at the moment, if they had made love and if so, how many times and with what degree of satisfaction compared to his own efforts. She was certainly not being as noisy as she was with him, but perhaps she was simply being discreet, or possibly the excessive enthusiasm was staged especially for his benefit.

Finally he got up, lit a cigarette and walked to the edge of the cliff. A few lights were still visible in the town below. He wondered if one of them belonged to their room in the hotel, if Dorothy was lying there thinking about him and missing him. He felt a sudden surge of longing for her and tried to drive it away by telling himself cynically that she was doubtless off somewhere in bed with Luigi, but the ache returned and he was unable to rid himself of a sense of regret and anger at his own foolishness. It was madness for him to be here with a woman who cared nothing for him, in the middle of a bunch of drunken maniacs and killers. He would go back tomorrow, he would apologise to Dorothy, she would forgive him, they would be reconciled and nothing like this would ever happen again. He took a last drag at his cigarette and flicked the still-burning stub over the edge of the cliff, watching as it trailed away out of sight into the trees below.

It proved far less easy for him to leave, however, than he had imagined. When he announced that he planned to depart by noon, Walter told him brusquely that he was a "guest" and that there was much more for him to see. "We wish to have the exceptional pleasure of your company for some time longer," he said.

"I suppose that means I'm a hostage or a prisoner of some kind," he accused Eva once he got her alone. "Was that your idea in bringing me here?"

"Of course not. Walter wants you to take part in something important later on today. After that, you can go whenever you want."

"What about you?"

"I'll stay. Walter says our enemies are planning a surprise attack, probably in a day or two. It's my duty to be here to help."

Feeling that he could no longer trust her, he thought of simply appropriating the car and driving off, but when he tried to approach it, he was warned away by a thuggish-looking guard who made threatening gestures with his rifle. Surely he could be of little use to them as a hostage, he thought: He was of no particular importance and abducting him might only damage relations with the foreign powers who had managed so successfully to avoid any involvement in the conflict to date. On the other hand, he thought gloomily, he was probably so insignificant that no one would ever consider his fate serious enough to warrant any kind of outside intervention.

The sound of shouting drew him back to the centre of the camp, where a group of soldiers were escorting a man who had been dragged out of the small, windowless hut; the other men were yelling abuse and gesticulating angrily, though they kept their distance and made no attempt to attack him. Working his way into the crowd, Roger recognised that the man was indeed the landlord of his hotel—though he was now a pitiful, terrified figure, his arms pinioned behind his back, his face bruised and covered with dried blood, his eyes darting back and forward among the spectators as he gabbled what were obviously pleas for mercy. Catching sight of Roger, he gaped in disbelief, then managed to break free from his captors and force his way far enough into the crowd to fall on his knees at Roger's feet. He was immediately seized again and hauled off towards one of the larger huts, still straining to look back at Roger and begging for assistance.

As the door slammed shut behind them, Roger realised that Eva was standing at his side. "I'd move away from here, if I were you," she warned quietly. "Our men don't look too kindly on friends of people like that scum." And indeed they were glaring at him with obvious hostility and muttering to one another.

He took her advice and moved hastily away. "I'm not a friend of his," he protested, "I'm not on anyone's side here. You all disgust me equally." There was a sudden, chilling scream of utter terror and pain from the hut, diverting the soldiers' attention from Roger as they nodded approvingly and moved closer in order to hear better. He noticed that Eva too was smiling. Another, even worse scream followed.

"Can't you stop them? Can't they just kill him and get it over with?"

"That would be too easy," she observed dreamily. "He has a lot to atone for before he dies."

"Then, for Christ's sake, help me to get out of here. I promise I won't tell anyone what's been going on. All I want to do is to get home and forget that any of this ever happened."

"You can leave in good time, *our* good time. But first you have a part to play in all this. Later on, this evening. They'll keep him alive till then."

He stared at her in astonished disbelief. "Is that what you brought me here for? To watch you kill him?"

"No, I brought you here in the hope that you would understand better what is going on here. But you're just like all the others, prejudiced and closed-minded. You don't even *want* to understand. This man shows you his photograph, he boasts about what he did, he even puts it on display. Why do you feel sorry for him?"

"He's still a human being." As if in confirmation of his comment, a roar of sheer agony emerged from the hut; the soldiers clustered around it had now been joined by their women and all were laughing and chatting excitedly.

"Look," she said, "he carried another photograph around with him. We found it in his pocket. Do you want to see it?" Without waiting for an answer, she showed it to him: a severed head, the features contorted in agony, a cigarette thrust mockingly into a corner of the half-open mouth. "That was another of his victims, another relative of Walter's, also killed with a saw. Do you still feel sorry for him?"

"I don't know. This is all beyond me. All I know is that no one deserves to suffer like this, even if he has made other people suffer. Just don't make me watch whatever you do tonight."

"We'll see."

"If you won't let me leave, at least let me get out of earshot."

"Go wherever you want. But the men have instructions to stop you if you go too far down the road."

He found his way as far as the caves without interference and sat on the plateau, staring over the scene below. Whatever happened, he vowed, he would not degrade himself by taking part in any further torture that might be inflicted on that wretched man tonight. He wondered why the obviously eager soldiers were being denied full involvement in what was going on just now; perhaps the intention was to whet their appetite for the final stages this evening. He thought too about Eva: Had she planned something like this from the beginning, or had a mild flirtation suddenly taken on a dangerous and unpredictable momentum of its own? Which was her real identity: the breathlessly adoring ingenue, the femme fatale, the coldhearted flirt, the sexual athlete, the righteous avenger of past wrongs, the hotblooded patriot? And had he ever been more than a puppet for her in any of these roles?

If Adam was right, it was perhaps possible to make his way through the caves to safety on the other side, but it would be madness to risk this without some kind of guide. Even so, might it not be more honourable at least to make the attempt, even if it ended in death by starvation, than to wait here passively till he was summoned possibly to inflict yet more pain on the pathetic creature who had fallen at his feet begging vainly for help? For they might demand more of him than simply providing a witness for whatever tortures they had in mind. Perhaps he could hide in one of the caves, avoiding discovery till they gave up the search and had their fun with the landlord without his presence. After dark he might be able to make his way down the hillside and back to town unobserved.

On the other hand, he realised, this might all be nothing but a nightmare, more vivid and consistent than those he had endured shortly after his arrival here, but ultimately no more truthful. If he struggled hard enough, he would be able to wake from it. He and Dorothy would never have come to this terrible place, they would be safely back home, he would wake up as usual and get ready to set off for work. He fought to rouse himself and, lulled by the hot sun and the sleepless night he had endured, fell soundly asleep.

He was wakened by a hand on his shoulder, shaking him roughly. One of the soldiers was staring down at him; when he saw Roger was awake, he hauled him to his feet. Three other men stood nearby; they grouped themselves silently around him and, after a push to put him in motion, set off back to the camp. His head felt fuzzy and his movements were uncoordinated; he stumbled several times and would have fallen at least once if one of the men had not seized his arm. It seemed to be evening already and the sun was low in the sky, though the air still felt warm and sticky. He glanced at his watch, but found that it had stopped exactly at noon. His mouth was dry and he was very hungry, having refused another helping of the anonymous stew this morning. He asked one of the men for a drink, gesturing towards his water bottle; the man handed it to him and he took a long swallow, realising too late that it contained brandy, not water. He gagged, spitting it out, as the man laughed at his discomfort, but the taste remained with him, burning his throat and increasing his thirst to such an extent that by the time they reached the camp, he felt delirious and could barely stand upright when the men pushed him into the middle of a circle formed by the rest of the inhabitants.

For what seemed a very long time, nothing much happened. The people around him were silent, occasionally shuffling their feet or clearing their throats. He could see no sign of either Walter or Eva. When he discovered that he could not stand any longer, he sat down, squatting with his legs crossed under him. As the sun finally edged out of sight below the horizon, those surrounding him began to set light to wooden torches soaked in pitch that they were carrying. In the flickering glare that these created against the encroaching darkness he made out a procession advancing towards him: Walter, Eva, four men carrying a plank or stretcher with something lying on it, other men holding variously shaped pieces of wood.

Walter motioned for him to stand up and he edged himself painfully to his feet. The men carrying the wood quickly erected a trestle table and the plank was laid on top of it; strapped to it was the landlord, stripped to the waist, his head rolling restlessly from side to side, his eyes wide open in terror. Roger realised with horror that one of the men was carrying a large double-handed saw; he set the saw upright on the ground, with his arms folded on the top handle and his chin propped against his wrists. His eyes met Roger's and he smiled almost imperceptibly.

Catching sight of the saw, the landlord began to scream, a low-pitched monotonous sound that seemed drained of any emotion and that quickly became irritating, rather than arousing feelings of pity and concern. Thank God, this is all a dream, Roger thought dully, as Walter took him by the arm, guided him towards the man holding the saw and positioned his fingers round the top handle. The man moved smoothly to the other side of the table, now holding the lower handle, so that the saw ended up poised directly above the landlord's body.

Once again there was a long pause as Roger waited for the moment when he would wake up, but when nothing happened, he dropped his end of the saw and turned to face Walter. The landlord uttered a yell of anguish as the blade scraped briefly against his flesh, and the second man continued to balance it in place over him.

"You must be crazy," Roger said. "You know I can't do this." He looked to Eva for support, but she met his gaze calmly and said nothing. "I'm getting out of here." He turned and began to walk away.

Two men holding rifles immediately stepped forward to block his path. "All right," Walter conceded. "I just thought you would have enjoyed it—I heard you had a taste for this kind of thing. If it worries you, why don't you end it for him quickly instead?"

One of the men pushed his rifle into Roger's hands; his fingers closed on it automatically while his brain continued to deny that any of this could really be taking place. "I can't do this," he repeated dully. "I can't kill him."

"It's that or the saw. Any of us would shoot him, even the women. Perhaps especially the women." When Roger made no response, Eva spoke up, her voice reasonable and even-tempered: "It's easy enough. Just put the barrel to his temple and pull the trigger. It'll be over in a second. Otherwise you'll have to watch him being cut in half and listen to him screaming. It won't be very pleasant. Walter's determined to have him killed one way or the other; why don't you help him to die easily and painlessly?" When he still said nothing, she added, her tone urgent and impatient now: "For God's sake, you fool, it took me hours to persuade Walter to do it this way. Do you want to ruin everything?"

He looked at the face of the man lying before him, mouth working soundlessly, eyes frantic with terror. Slowly, he placed the barrel of the rifle against the landlord's forehead. Then, with what seemed infinite slowness, he swivelled it round till it was pointing at Walter. "Let him go," he said, his mouth so dry that the words could scarcely be heard and he had to repeat them. "Set him free."

For a moment time stood still and he wondered why the guard beside him did not attempt to shoot him and why Walter's hand seemed scarcely to move as it snaked towards him and finally, after several centuries, plucked the rifle from his grasp. His finger tightened on the trigger and met empty air, and now Walter was pointing the gun at him, his mouth set in a crooked smile, and another infinity went by as Roger waited for him to fire.

Walter's whitening knuckle closed on the trigger with a faint click, and sound and motion returned with a rush as Roger found himself sprawled on the ground with Walter standing over him roaring with laughter. "No bullets!" he shouted, showing him the empty magazine. "You didn't think I'd trust you with real bullets? It was all just a joke!"

Roger rose slowly to his feet as the bystanders rocked with laughter, though their response seemed good-natured rather than malicious. He had put on a good show for them, an attempted gesture of integrity that had turned out to be both futile and ridiculous, and they were happy to show their appreciation. He had no idea whether the landlord was in on the joke too, but the man had been set free and now sat cautiously on the edge of the table, smiling weakly.

The crowd began to disperse, still chuckling and talking animatedly. Roger saw Eva approaching him and, to avoid her, set off rapidly towards the tent. A few torches still flickered in the night breeze, but most had been extinguished and the main illumination was provided by the stars and the thin sliver of a new moon. He found his holdall and began to throw into it the few items of clothing he had pulled out of it; as he finished, he found Eva standing beside him.

"Go away," he told her. "Leave me alone. Haven't you done enough damage?"

"I didn't know he was going to do that. He tricked me too. He must have found out about you and me, or guessed it anyway, and wanted to humiliate you. I thought I was acting for the best. I'm sorry."

"Acting for the best in trying to turn me into a murderer?"

"It was either that or watching the man get cut in half. Or possibly skinned alive—that was another alternative."

"You didn't feel very sorry for him this morning. You said he deserved to die."

"Die, yes. But not like that."

"So what will happen to him now?"

"It's happened already. Walter cut his throat." Responding to his start of horror, she added sharply: "You didn't think we'd let him go free, did you? Not after everything he'd done. If you like, you can give yourself credit for his having died quickly."

"Credit," he repeated, as if in a daze, "Do you think I would want to take *credit* for that?"

"As you wish." She was clearly losing interest in the matter. "You can leave tomorrow now, whenever you want. Go back to your little wife. You'll have a lot to tell her about."

"Did you ever feel anything for me at all?" he asked.

"Of course I did," she said. "But you spoiled it."

He spent the rest of the night lying on the ground, wrapped in a blanket, as far away from the others as he could get. He saw neither Eva nor Walter the next morning before he left, but one of the women cooking breakfast offered him some of the porridge-like mixture that she was preparing. Despite the terrible taste and smell, he swallowed it ravenously and even accepted a second helping. No one was guarding the car and the key was in the ignition; as he started it, he noticed that the fuel gauge was low and hoped that he had enough to take him back to town. The sun was high in the sky already and he found it impossible to judge the time, though it was probably well after eight. The hands of his watch still indicated noon.

He drove past the path leading to the caves and wondered what would have happened if he had succeeded in hiding there after all. Would they really have killed their victim in that barbaric way, or was the whole thing just an elaborate hoax to which he had succumbed? Could he even trust Eva when she said that Walter had finished off the landlord? He could believe little else that she had told him. Perhaps the landlord was an ally rather than an enemy, willingly helping to humiliate a gullible foreigner. In any event, he must put the whole thing behind him, like a bad dream whose contents would soon fade and dissolve and be forgotten. He had done nothing wrong, he had killed nobody, he had even tried to save a man's life at the expense of his own. He had often speculated on how he would cope with a truly extreme situation, like that his father had been forced to suffer through, and he felt at least he had not disgraced himself. He would tell Dorothy everything about it, not omitting anything, and perhaps she would feel proud of him. Once he got back to town, he would insist that they leave as soon as possible. He would say he was sorry, he had learned his lesson, nothing like this would ever happen again. And it wouldn't.

He drove more confidently now, taking the bends with ease, thinking of the welcome he would receive.

⧉ Margaret ⧉

I keep thinking about Dimitrios and his strange ideas about multiple universes, each virtually identical with the next but with one or two apparently minor changes that, cumulatively, reverberate to change the course of history. Move into the universe next door, and everything seems familiar at first, until, slowly, you realise that this is not *your* world after all—a person whom you think you recognise now has a different name and her life has subtly altered; a town you lived in no longer exists, or is now in another country; the world, in short, takes a slight tilt, making you dizzy, and when it settles down again the contours are alien, yet seemingly the same. Or, to put it another way, it is as if you turned the page of a book to find that page exactly repeated, everything predictable, everything familiar—except for two or three words, and these words change everything. And in the universe beyond that, the differences are correspondingly greater, affecting the destiny not just of individuals, but of countries, continents, empires. Ridiculous, of course, and surely pointless, but—as Dimitrios argued—a logical consequence of the idea of infinity and not impossible if you accept that.

And is it really all that strange if you consider the multiple possibilities each of us faces at each moment of our lives, the random accidents of birth and upbringing, the chance encounters that cause us to meet one person rather than another, to make this choice rather than that—and then the ripples spreading from each of these and interacting with the other endless currents from the lives of other people—so that if you could somehow allow each person to experience all the possibilities open at any moment, we would indeed have an infinite number of lives, some almost identical, others unimaginably different. And yet, in some sense too, these would also be lives that we *choose*—not totally, not always freely, but never simply as helpless puppets, jerking to the strings that we can never control and sometimes cannot even see, but to which we respond nonetheless. Nothing ever really comes to an end: There is always another possibility open, another choice, another train missed or caught, another sequence of events following from that. And I would like to believe Dimitrios—though I cannot—when he says that death is never final, just another shifting of the earth and, when it settles down again, there we are, living another of our endlessly potential lives.

Lives that echo, overlap, run parallel, interact. I can imagine another self, reading this perhaps centuries in the future, saying to herself: "This is what *I* feel, I too have thought and suffered like this, I have lost a child, a lover, I have felt a similar joy in the act of creation, a similar grief at the brutality and cruelty that seem inescapable whatever place and time and universe we live in"—though, to haul in Dimitrios once again, there must be *some* world where people manage to arrange things better than they do here and we should all have our turn at living in it. If there is, however, we seem to manage to forget it very quickly. And I can imagine another self too, a self in the past, who thought and felt all these things, and, if I were ever to encounter her, I would recognise myself in her as well.

But all this is heresy and would condemn me totally if any one should read it. So I have written it in a language of my own devising, one that should baffle those out there already baying for my blood, but not so indecipherable that someone, sometime, somewhere, with the sympathy and patience to search for it, should not find the key.